Scorpion

Sons of the Sheikh

Book 1

Mel Teshco

Scorpion

Cover Art by HelzKat Designs
https://www.helzkatdesigns.com/

Chapter One

Sheikh Aziz Al-Hadid stalked through the market in his traditional thobe and keffiyeh headdress, his gaze sweeping left and right through the crowd as he searched for the one woman who'd evaded him for too long already.

Two years, four months, six days to be exact, but who was counting?

He smiled grimly as he thrust aside some scarves hanging from a rack, dust billowing off the colorful fabrics thanks to the desert sands that lifted sporadically in the air from oven-hot breezes.

Not that he was focused on the state of the market stalls. He was here for Zamira Fasih, only daughter of Sheikh Cairo, ruler of Qadania. The neighboring country bordered Aziz's Middle East province, Mukaite.

That he and Cairo were hostiles, thanks to Aziz's late father choosing sides with the wrong friend—Cairo's enemy—meant Aziz had been forbidden to even go near Zamira let alone date her. He sighed heavily. He couldn't see that restriction lifting anytime soon, if ever.

His father might have died two years ago, but the hate he'd left behind still ran deep. Sheikh Cairo would never forget or forgive the betrayal of Aziz's father—Cairo's once close friend.

A brown-and-white goat bleated just ahead, the bell around its neck jangling as a shepherd led the animal through the market by a rope attached to its collar. The rest of the small herd followed behind.

A vendor frowned at the animals as he peddled his colorful floor rugs, while a local farmer nearby seemed oblivious to everything and everyone as he finished setting up his stall of produce, which included organic coffee, olive oil and Mukaite honey.

Aziz strode past the vendors and bleating animals as he headed toward the pens where the goats would be locked away and sold. But it wasn't the goat pens where he guessed he'd find Zamira. He'd be much more likely to find her at the yards where quality camels waited to be sold.

She was obsessed with the big animals and traveled for miles to see and buy quality stock. He'd personally selected a few of his best bulls and cows to ensure the right people passed on information to the right buyers...namely Zamira. Word of mouth was critical in his goal to entice her across the border onto his land.

Though Qadania skirted this part of his province, she knew better than most not to step onto Mukaite soil.

It was still his land.

His territory. His rules.

He turned a corner between more vendor stalls, momentarily out of sight of his guards who trailed behind him. They were trained to be silent and unobtrusive, and to blend into the crowd.

He might have loads of perks being a sheikh, but his lack of privacy wasn't one of them. He itched to be alone and completely free, but only a fool would do that with so many wishing him harm thanks to the Qadania war.

He drew in a steadying breath, the meaty, smoky scent of grilled lamb shish kebabs filling his lungs. He quickened his pace through the crowded route that led him directly toward the camels. He was perhaps twenty or thirty yards away when he spied the big yellow, cream and brown animals ahead.

His breath caught and he slowed as his gaze narrowed, his world centering on Zamira as she stood in the middle of the large, unpredictable animals. His pulse surged, an expletive bursting through his gritted teeth.

What had he expected? She'd never been a softly-spoken, demure princess. She was bold and daring and had never shown fear around camels. And though her confidence was one of the many things he found attractive, right then it took everything he had not to shout at her to get out to the safety on the other side of the post and rail fencing.

He took a deep, calming breath. This was the perfect opportunity to study her while she was in her element and completely unaware of him, to see if the war really *had* affected her—at least outwardly—as much as what his spies had told him it had.

No. She looked the same, more beautiful, if anything.

Though her lithe body was concealed beneath a modest navy and white abaya, and her gorgeous, long dark hair with its streaks of burnished copper was hidden behind a navy hijab, her sparkling, honey-dark eyes and nose with its tilted tip, as well as her heart-shaped face were more than enough to showcase her beauty.

She was utter perfection.

He slowed his pace, taking his time to admire her while she was happy and at her most natural. He'd bet that'd change the moment she became aware of him.

She blamed him as much as she had his late father for the war that caused her people to suffer. She hated him even more for not stopping it.

His chest compressed. He'd been working behind the scenes to do just that, but there was more to it than simply requesting Sheikh Idris to pull his soldiers out of the country where he'd been pillaging all its resources, namely its black gold. Nothing and no one would stop Idris from enjoying his spoils.

Well...almost nothing, and Aziz refused to go down that road.

Call him selfish, but he enjoyed his freedom far too much to surrender it anytime soon. His sheikha mother might not have been his biological mom, but he'd loved her more than anyone else in the world. He refused to suffer like she had from being in a loveless, arranged marriage.

He stopped at the yards, resting his arms on the top railing and watching as Zamira stroked the chocolate-brown neck of Aziz's most prized bull. Did she know who owned the camel? Then her words floated his way, confirming she did.

"Your master is a fool to let you get away, but then he's a fool about a lot of things, isn't he?"

The camel grunted, as though in agreement, and Aziz couldn't stop his wry grin as he eavesdropped.

"You'll be coming home with me today, then put to work making big, strong strapping babies. I'm sure you won't complain though." Her hand stopped its soothing strokes. "I bet your master doesn't complain either when he's busy doing the same thing."

Aziz cocked a brow. "I'm not sure where you've been getting your information from, but I'm certainly *not* going around trying to make babies."

She jumped and gasped, her voice accusing as she swung around to face him. "What are you doing here?" Her golden-brown eyes darkened. "And what are you doing listening in on a private conversation?"

"Why *wouldn't* I be here? I own this bit of land you're standing on. As for a private conversation, nothing is less private than when you're out in the open gossiping about me to one of my camels."

"Well Butch knows how to keep a secret. I'm just sorry I spoke in your vicinity."

Butch? His lips twitched some more. The male camel was a pedigree worth his weight in gold. That the bull had also just happened to have won his last five races meant his value had easily tripled. He wasn't sure "Butch" cut it as a name.

Aziz lifted a hand and ran his fingertips through his neatly trimmed beard. "I'm glad you did," he said huskily. "It's given me a chance to clear my name."

She huffed out a laugh as she stepped toward him, then said in a brittle undertone, "You might fool your people into believing you're some kind of virtuous demigod, but you don't fool me. You have a smeared name for good reason."

His muscles tensed, his shoulders going so rigid he wondered if they'd snap. "For good reason?" he repeated softly.

"While your people enjoy their quality lifestyle," she swept a hand toward the sandy ridge behind her, "my people are barely scraping together an existence thanks to the evil sheikh you support!"

"I can't reverse the contract my father signed in good faith...the same contract that keeps my people safe."

"Of course you can't," she sneered. "While your province flourishes along with your people, you'll happily turn a blind eye to what is happening to your neighbors."

"Believe what you want," he said in an even tone, though anger sparked deep inside. She'd totally misjudged him. "You'll soon imagine the worst of me anyway."

She huffed out a laugh. "How could I possibly imagine worse of you than what I already do?" She tossed her head, the long end of her hijab slipping behind a shoulder. "This conversation is over." She waved some men over who were clearly her bodyguards, their thobes doing little to hide their firearms. "I'll make sure this will be the last time we meet."

"It's a bit late for that," he countered, waving his own bodyguards forward, the same ones who'd discreetly trailed behind him in the markets. That he had at least three times as many men as she did was obvious by the way her bodyguards froze, then looked nervously at one another. "This is just the start of what will be a long and fruitful relationship."

She spun around, her mouth dropping open. "What are you talking about?"

He smirked, his conscience taking a holiday at the knowledge she'd soon be his. "You're coming with me."

Chapter Two

Zamira's pulse thundered in her ears, her mind for a moment forgetting everything but the charismatic man in front of her. The one and same man she hated and wanted all at the same time.

But what woman *wouldn't* want him? He hypnotized the opposite sex with his designer stubble that covered his strong jaw and high cheekbones, his crisp white thobe that outlined more than covered his tall, strong and corded body. Even his slightly beaked nose suited his aristocratic face with its high cheekbones and firm lips, his dark almost black eyes. Not to mention his white keffiyeh that was in stark contrast to his tanned face and throat.

Ugh. She should have known better than to come here, but she'd snuck over the border to view the prime camels that she so badly wanted to add to her breeding stock. That a piece of her had hoped to run into Aziz, no matter how unlikely, had added to her desire to leave her country for a short time.

She should have known better. He wasn't called Scorpion for nothing. His sting really was lethal.

And what about the man you've promised to marry?

She flinched, her stomach hardening. She'd been doing an amazing job so far of *not* thinking about her impending marriage. But soon enough she'd have no choice but to face reality. She only wished she was attracted to Rahim like she was attracted to Aziz.

Rahim's integrity was her only real consolation prize in all this. He might not be charming or overly handsome, but at least he was willing to step up to the plate to fight a war that Qadania was currently losing.

She swallowed hard, her pulse thudding faintly in her ears. That she'd have to marry him was a small price to pay to protect her people.

The captain of her guards stepped forward and she put a hand up to stop him. The last thing she wanted was for one of her friends to be killed trying to defend her. "It's okay, Ali. Sheikh Aziz won't hurt me."

She hoped. Her judgement wasn't exactly up to par when it came to him.

"Hurting you is the last thing I want," Aziz acknowledged as he gestured for her to climb out of the yard. When she reluctantly did so, he held out his hand. "Give me your phone."

"You can't be serious?"

"Do I look like I'm joking?" he asked.

She held his gaze for a good ten seconds before she reached into the pocket of her abaya and withdrew her phone. "Here," she gritted out.

He took it from her then nodded at her captain of the guards before he threw it to him. "You can give that back to her when she returns."

The captain nodded before Aziz curled his fingers around her forearm and drew her close.

She stifled a gasp at the electricity zapping through her nerve endings. Did he feel it too? Or was their connection only one-sided?

His lips tightened before he glanced at Ali. "Tell your sheikh I'll return her within the week...if she wants to return."

She snorted. "If you think for a second I'll want to stay you have rocks in your head." She dragged her stare away from the man who left her weak-kneed and all too self-aware thanks to his charisma and power. Holding Ali's shell-shocked stare, she said, "Tell my father coming here was all my idea, and that you presumed I'd gotten permission to attend the camel sale."

He shook his head. "I can't—"

"That's an order," she cut in. "I-I'll be fine. I'll see you in a week."

Her captain's face paled. "If you come back with your innocence lost, your father will—"

"Tell her father not to worry," Aziz interjected. "Her hymen will remain intact. A physician can confirm that easily enough."

The captain nodded grimly before Aziz drew her away from him and the rest of her men and toward his own. They surrounded her and Aziz before he stalked with her out of the bustling market and its staring people and toward a fleet of big black SUVs.

She resisted wrenching her arm free and instead asked tightly, "Where are you taking me?"

He cocked a brow. "To my palace. You'll be extremely comfortable there." He chuckled darkly. "Did you think I'd take you to some fleapit?"

She almost stumbled before he steadied her easily with his grip. "I don't know," she conceded. She looked up at him, her heart beating even faster to find his dark stare already on her. She gulped. "I used to think you were the nicest of the brothers, turned out I was wrong."

He waited until she climbed into the back seat then slid in beside her before he answered. "Don't judge me just because my province is the only one that backs onto your country."

"We're neighbors," she hissed. She clipped on her seatbelt, then put as much space between herself and him as the belt permitted. "You should have done something to help!"

He stiffened. "It's on my to-do list."

She bit back an expletive, her emotions threatening to shatter. Did he have no consideration towards her country's suffering? To *her* suffering?

And to think the last time she'd met him she'd developed a major crush on him. Not even his four handsome brothers—all adopted after the sheikh of Turain realized he was infertile—could outshine Aziz.

In her eyes he'd been flawless.

The driver followed a pair of the fleet of cars—two in front and two in back—out of the market and down the asphalt road sprinkled generously with sand.

She'd never been to his palace, he'd had it built after his father had been on his deathbed and had divided the country of Turain up into provinces so that all his sons had their own piece of land along with the people in it.

She had no doubt the palace would be beautiful, just like its owner.

Aziz and his brothers knew how to make money while keeping their people happy and their provinces at peace. A pity Aziz hadn't extended even a little of that goodwill into her war torn country, Qadania.

She stared out the passenger window and watched the world go past, or at least, the part of the world that was Mukaite. It was all sand and dunes, with sporadic bits of flora including the twisted white trunks and startling greenery of juniper trees, the blue-gray saltbush, and some clusters of date palms.

"I'm not the monster you think I am," Aziz said softly.

She did her best to ignore him before she forced herself to turn and look up at his breathtaking good looks. "I'm certain only a monster would kidnap a woman and take her away from her own country and family."

"If it makes you feel any better, I meant what I said earlier. I won't be taking your virginity. I'm only borrowing you for a week."

"Why?" she choked out. "What do you hope to achieve?"

"Other than making you realize I'm not the bad guy?"

"You will never convince me otherwise," she said bitterly. "There is a reason they call you Scorpion. No one could sting so many like you have."

"You say that like you know me." His eyes glinted, his voice rasping. "Perhaps this week will help to change your mind about me."

"In your dreams," she said with a snort. "Nothing will make me change my mind about you."

"We shall see," he said quietly.

"Yes, we shall." She turned away from him, disturbed by his conviction. She was even more disturbed by the doubts creeping into her psyche when he'd already proven just how selfish he really was.

Her war torn country and hollow-eyed people were proof of that.

Chapter Three

Aziz wanted to ground his teeth together. But he refused to defend himself by a whole bunch of words that were meaningless without the proof to back them. She needed to witness his good deeds and come to her own realization that he wasn't the villain she believed him to be.

Not that he was pure of heart, either. He'd done things he wasn't proud of, things that had benefitted him and his people.

Like ignoring the Qadania war?

He winced. He hadn't ignored it, exactly. Trying to get Sheikh Idris to do anything, unless it benefitted his own agenda, was like pissing into a strong wind and not getting wet. It was near impossible.

He reached for her hand, her fingers immediately stiffening under his clasp. He stroked his thumb back and forth across her palm, enjoying the tingles of electricity that jolted through him. Little wonder he was so attracted to her, had always been attracted to her, the magic between them was undeniable.

"What is this all about?" she asked suddenly. "I mean, why kidnap me? My father already despises you and your family. He'll hate you a hundred times more now."

He shrugged. "It was his hatred that didn't allow me to see you in the first place. I had to take matters into my own hands."

She jerked her hand free and sniggered, the sound too close to hysteria. "You really are spoilt, aren't you? You couldn't get what you wanted, so you took it anyway. I hope you're proud of yourself."

He frowned. She made him sound like some overindulged brat. "When I want something, I work hard to get it. It's as simple as that."

Her smooth brow creased as she stared at him. "So you're saying this whole kidnapping thing was a setup? You planned everything?"

He nodded. "I knew you couldn't resist checking out my best camels, especially my bull, so I made sure they were at the market's sale yards."

She slumped against her seat. "I was so naïve," she admitted dully.

"You had no reason to believe you wouldn't be safe." He couldn't help but rush to reassure her. "You had your guards."

"They had no chance against all your men," she said bitterly. "As it was I had very few to spare, not while most of them are off fighting a war."

His chest tightened. How had she made her war become his in just a few words? Everything he'd done had been for the benefit of his people and he refused to feel shame for keeping them safe.

She sniffled before conceding, "I've had my eye on Butch for a while now...ever since he won his first race. He might be the most impressive camel I've seen yet."

"I don't doubt that," Aziz said. "He's the product of a lot of selective breeding."

"Product?" Her lips curled. "Of course you'd turn a living thing into an asset. Everything comes down to cash for you, doesn't it?"

Aziz shrugged. If she wanted to turn his every word into an accusation, then so be it. He'd play along with her. "Without cash my province and my people would be impoverished."

Her eyes flashed. "War has a funny way of making that happen." She tilted her head to the side. "I guess you can only hope and pray that you never experience it for yourself."

He pushed away the unsettling idea. "I've done everything in my power to see that it doesn't."

Her eyes narrowed and he withheld a sigh. It was time for a subject change. "My palace is just over the crest of that hill." He nodded toward the windshield; the pair of SUV's at the front already climbing the incline. "It's a sight to behold."

She looked ahead. It wasn't until their car breached the top that her eyes widened and she gasped. "That's yours?"

He smiled at the white palace spread out below with its domes that were outlined in gold, date palms flanking the sides of the palace and a pool of water at its front reflecting the stunning architecture.

"It is," he acknowledged. "As I said, you'll be more than comfortable there."

She arched a brow. "I can't imagine being comfortable sleeping on a solid gold bed."

"Then luckily for you there are no gold beds in the palace, though I'm sure it could be arranged."

She snorted but otherwise didn't say anything more as they approached his palace. Black, ornamental gates that were tipped in gold slid apart as the convoy of SUV's neared and then drove through.

The lake glinted like a mirage on one side as they headed toward the palace before veering right, the driveway then cutting between land and water. Shrubbery that had been clipped into hedges lined either side of the road before joining in a semi-circle ahead. The vehicles stopped at the dead-end, the driver abandoning his seat to open the back passenger door.

She didn't move for a good handful of seconds, her whole body stiffening in defiance. Then she seemed to realize there was no point in defying Aziz and making it harder on herself. With a dejected sigh, she climbed out of the seat.

He alighted behind her, following her gaze to where she'd noticed the gap in the hedges. It verged on being a secret entrance, which allowed people access to the palace via the marble steps leading up to imposing white pillars that were also tipped with gold.

She stood, dazed like a little mouse in a tall and inescapable cage. Then he took her hand and drew her with him through the hedges and onto the thick marble steps. "This way," he murmured.

Sand particles rolled along the steps as they ascended them. She smiled, no doubt amused to find his palace wasn't completely perfect.

He bent a little and informed, "The sand makes the stairs less slippery."

"Of course it does," she said, apparently peeved that Mother Nature herself had solved his problem. "I suppose my kidnapping had been planned with the same foresight?"

He stopped beneath the pillars that soared into the sky, turning to look down at her. "Did you imagine I slapped it together in a matter of seconds?" He shook his head. "I don't do things half-assed." His voice turned husky. "Especially with those things that are so important to me."

Her eyes went dewy, her breathing a little erratic. Until she snapped out of it and turned hostile once again. "I wasn't aware I was a *thing*."

He cupped her face and swooped low, his lips sliding over hers. At first she stiffened, her body unresponsive. It didn't take long before she became pliant and willing, her lips softening under his and her arms twining around his neck.

She tasted like cinnamon and vanilla, her skin and lips as silken and soft as rose petals. He drew in a whiff of lavender—her shampoo?—before he reluctantly pulled back. Though he wanted desperately to continue kissing her, there was a time and place for that, where no guards were looking on and where privacy was in no doubt.

She blinked up at him, the tip of her tongue sliding across her top lip as though to taste him. His pulse escalated, need thrumming through him. He stepped back. He'd promised that her hymen would stay intact and so far he hadn't shown great resistance in that regard.

"Is that why I'm here?" she asked hoarsely, her eyes round. "So that you can have fun with the virgin sheikha?"

He shook his head, and stated bluntly, "You're here because I know you are to wed another." He held her narrowed stare. "And I'm running out of time to change your mind."

Chapter four

Zamira wasn't sure whether to laugh or cry. Not least because she'd never resort to choosing Aziz over a man who was willing to do everything, including marrying her, to stop the war. Even if she wasn't attracted to the man. "Rahim is honorable."

Aziz's mouth slackened. Then he shook his head and queried, "Unlike me?"

"I never said that."

"Not directly, but it was implied."

"You *did* kidnap me." She sucked in a harsh breath and put a hand to her chest as the consequences of what Aziz did dawned on her. "Rahim might refuse my hand in marriage now thanks to you."

"Then he's not worthy of you." He drew her with him beneath the grand portico and toward intricately carved double doors, where guards in thobes stood like statues before they moved to open the doors.

He nodded at his men as he walked through the doorway with her. As they respectfully bowed their heads in return, she had to resist not scowling at them or sticking out her tongue. Anything to make them react and not look like they worshipped the ground Aziz walked on.

She supposed most of his people adored him while peace and productivity continued in his province.

Then they were stepping into a cavernous space where blue had been added to the white and gold theme thanks to intricately patterned mosaic tiles that covered the floor and walls, and the huge cavity above that revealed a domed skylight. Enormous teardrop-shaped chandeliers hung either side of the skylight, the shimmering crystals emphasizing the sheer size of the room.

"I host many celebrations here. The room is convenient to say the least. Guests don't have to walk for miles getting lost while looking for the party. It can be a bit of maze."

"Impressive," she conceded before adding a little drily, "but perhaps a little excessive."

"Your palace is just as grand," he reminded.

She managed a tight smile. She'd almost forgotten he'd visited the Qadania palace a few times in the past, before their sheikh fathers had stopped being friends. The last time had been almost two and a half years ago, the visit one she'd been trying hard to forget.

She lifted her chin. She would *not* go down that road. "Much of my father's palace has been stripped of its treasures to help pay for our security. You're probably aware our crude oil was the first resource to be raided by Idris."

He nodded. "It's common knowledge." He escorted her farther into the room before taking a staircase to the level above. He stopped on the landing and nodded to his right. "You'll find most of the guest bedrooms and sitting rooms that way." He nodded to his left. "This way you'll find my office and bedroom suite."

"Which guest bedroom is mine?"

He shook his head. "You're not staying in any of the guest bedrooms. You're staying with me where I can keep an eye on you." He smiled grimly. "I don't for a second imagine you won't try to escape."

She gaped, her pulse thundering in her ears even as forbidden thoughts entered her head...his strong legs wrapped around her thighs, his mouth plundering hers while he plunged deep—

She cleared her throat, her voice coming out shrill as she said, "Assign me a guard then—two guards!—I cannot stay in your bedroom."

He lifted a hand and touched her face. "Don't be anxious. I promised I wouldn't break your hymen. I meant it."

She was too shocked, too stimulated to reply as he drew her with him to a wide corridor and through an arched opening where groupings of cozy armchairs surrounded low tables with books spread out on them. Single chairs in private nooks invited a more personal space for those who needed it.

"My sitting room," he said. "I often use this space for reading and relaxing."

She blinked as she looked around. In all her dreams and imaginings about this man, this hadn't been one of them. She'd had more...erotic thoughts. Her chest tightened. She didn't doubt for a moment he'd had plenty of sexual encounters, probably in this very room.

He might be a modern sheikh but he'd no doubt keep a harem—like so many of the older sheikhs did—to satisfy his perverted needs.

"I'm sure you'll lose yourself in many of the books here, both fiction and non-fiction." He bent and picked up a book on camels. "You might already have this one."

Her thoughts about his sex life slipped away as she smiled and nodded. "I do. But I'd happily read it again."

He put the book down, then led her toward another set of double doors, opening one of the carved, mahogany-stained doors and stepping into an opened suite of rooms that left her both spellbound and resentful. How must it feel not to watch your home being stripped of all its valuables just to survive?

She glanced to the right at the sunken floor where a couple of rows of comfy armchairs faced a curtained wall, the home theater part of the room, though she could see where a moveable section of wall slid across to make the theater darker and more private.

To the left a large kitchen with all the mod cons gleamed under downlights, a white marble island bench with swirls of blue and gold a gorgeous feature along with the white-cushioned, gold-metal bar stools pushed beneath an overhang.

Huge tinted windows led out to a balcony where the top fronds of date palms rustled ever so slightly in a breeze. The cloudless azure sky outside shimmered under the relentless sun, while inside it was cool thanks to ducted air conditioning that no doubt ran through the entire palace.

On the other side of the kitchen cream-cushioned chairs were tucked beneath a large mahogany table, which displayed orchids in a crystal vase. A long blue sofa and matching oversized armchairs with cream cushions were grouped around a large screen television.

He nodded at a corridor that opened up behind a far-off wall. "The two doors to the right are my office and my bedroom. The two doors to the left are my gym and library."

She had no choice but to follow him as he stalked down the corridor, then pushed the farthest door open to the right to reveal his bedroom. A masculine king-sized bed with a black velvet cover and crisp white pillows edged in black were the first things she noticed.

Her breathing seemed to grow shallow, her knees weakening and her mind becoming overactive as she envisioned what went on in the bed. Then she forced her stare away and took in the rest of the room.

A six-drawer dresser was built into the wall, an oval mirror reflecting a chandelier that gleamed like sunlit snow. A long cream chaise lounge was tucked next a window in front of overlong, sheer white voile curtains, while the mosaic floor and walls were far more understated in white with gold accents.

His palace was incredible.

"This way," he said, leading her through an opening at the end of the bedroom.

To the left she spied a wide opening that revealed a glimpse of the bathroom, where white tiles and a vanity showcased gold taps and a faucet. She couldn't see past the wall but imagined there would be a big bathtub or double shower behind it.

To the right was a walk-in wardrobe showcasing luxurious gray carpet on the floors. Nooks and crannies in the walls stored everything from shoes to aftershave and ties, underwear and socks. Thobes along with western shirts and pants hung on thick wooden hangers, and she couldn't resist stepping onto the carpet and running her hands along the expensive fabrics of his clothes.

"I've had women's clothes brought in for you," he said in a low, too intimate voice. "Abayas and hijabs along with western gowns, pants and tops. There are even some bikinis if you choose to use the pool outside."

"You have a pool?"

He nodded. "Of course. It's just outside the bedroom's balcony. Come, take a look."

She followed him back into the bedroom and through a set of tinted doors that slid aside and opened onto a large balcony with an intimate table and four cushioned chairs. Stairs led down to the end of an aqua pool that had to be at least twenty meters long. A trio of large sails covered most of it, preventing the sun from making the water hot or giving swimmers sunburn.

He smiled her way. "You won't be bored here."

"So this is—what? A vacation?"

"This whole week will be for you and me to get acquainted."

Chapter Five

Aziz tried to read the emotions flashing across Zamira's face, but they happened too fast to single out just one. If anything was clear, though, it was her absolute refusal at having to stay here against her will.

Not that he blamed her. He'd taken away her freedom by forcing her into his world. But he'd run out of options. She'd soon be married to another and he couldn't have that, not without putting up a fight. Besides, the man she was going to wed might put on a good front, but he was nothing more than a criminal, an underworld figure whose authority and power came from drugs and firearms.

That Zamira's father refused to believe anything bad about Rahim because he was willing to supply arms and fight their enemy to bring peace back to Qadania was just another reason for Aziz to kidnap Zamira and open her eyes to the truth.

She was making a terrible mistake marrying Rahim.

The man might have promised her the world, but he'd want ten times more back in return. He'd want her heart and her soul, and he'd have fun trying to bring her down to his level in the process.

Aziz reached up and brushed his fingertips across her smooth, flushed cheek. "I'll treat you like the princess you are while you're here."

She stiffened but didn't pull away. "And yet I'm still a prisoner."

He nodded. "I'm sorry it had to be that way."

"Just not sorry enough to change your mind and release me?"

He dropped his arm back to his side, his smile not from any sense of humor. He'd gambled everything to bring her here, not least possibly starting a war with her father. That the man was verging on impoverished from the present war with Sheikh Idris was possibly the only thing that would stop him from crossing into Mukaite with all guns blazing. "It was a risk worth taking," Aziz said simply.

She blinked up at him, as though trying to read his every thought. Good luck with that. He was known for being pokerfaced and not giving away his emotions or his strategies.

Speaking of which...did she had any idea how much thought he'd put into getting her to his palace? He'd gone through every move, every possible outcome in his mind before putting into place everything that needed to be done.

In the end it'd been simple. Lure her in...then take her.

"You must be hungry," he said, glancing at his gold wristwatch. It was beyond time for a subject change. "Let's eat lunch inside where it's cool."

She nodded and didn't object. He should have been relieved. If anything a rush of concern filled him, his chest tightening. She didn't do meek and obedient, she was a firecracker with a brilliant mind and a short fuse.

They went back inside and he closed the sliding door behind them. He didn't bother clicking the lock into place. He had guards assigned all around the palace. He hadn't gone to the trouble to kidnap her just for her to escape.

Heading to his bar, he filled two glasses with ice before picking up his gold *ibrik* to pour *arak* from its spout. The alcohol was made from grapes and aniseed, and as the clear liquid hit the ice, the drink turned a translucent milky-white.

He handed her a glass, then lifted his to clink them together before he murmured, "*Lana*."

"To us," she repeated in English, though her voice was as empty as her stare. She wasn't even trying to convince him she was prepared to go through the week with him.

Why would she? As far as she was concerned, he'd done everything but fire bullets at her people. He'd yet to prove himself an honorable man. She saw him as the enemy, as bad if not worse than Sheikh Idris.

She gulped down her drink. He took a small sip. Didn't she realize how potent *arak* was on an empty stomach? He grimaced. She was probably trying to become numb, immune to him and her present predicament.

He placed the *ibrik* on the dining table, then putting down his glass of *arak,* he pulled out a nearby chair and said, "take a seat."

"Thank you," she muttered before she dropped into the seat he'd chosen.

He pushed her closer to the table. "My chef will be here soon. I've already instructed him to send up some dishes to share."

"Are you certain they won't be poisoned?" she asked sweetly.

He hid a smirk. She might act sober but her eyes were already a little glazed.

"If it makes you feel better I'll take the first bite."

She swirled what was left of her milky-white drink, the aniseed scent filling the air and her ice clinking together. Then she tipped the remainder of the alcohol to her mouth and swallowed it in one mouthful.

He arched a brow. She'd be passed out on her chair before the food even arrived at this rate. Either that or she'd be spilling secrets and speaking her mind. He reached for the *ibrik* and poured some more *arak* into her glass.

He hoped it was the latter.

"Are you *trying* to get me drunk?" she asked, then shook her head and giggled before she added, "Whatever." She swallowed another large mouthful. "This is acshually really good." Draining the last of the liquid, she pushed her empty glass toward him. "More, *hic,* plea-shhe."

He didn't argue. He poured another good-sized splash into her glass while refraining from anymore for himself. Perhaps he was being too hard-hitting and aggressive in wanting to learn what he could from her, but a week would flash by all too quickly.

"So what does your dad say about me?" he queried lightly. Like this was nothing more than a little chitchat between friends.

She choked out a scornful laugh. "He says the apple doeshn't fall far from the tree. That all the Al-Hadid boys could have been Sheikh Rami's bi-bioligshical sons."

"And what do you say about that?"

She put her elbow on the table and leaned her chin on her upturned palm, her liquid honey eyes shining like condemning stars. "I think he'sh right."

Even though he knew her answer before she spoke the words it was still something of a kick to his stomach. But that was just one of the reasons he'd brought her here. He wanted to open her eyes so she could see things from his side of the world and maybe even begin to like him...more than like him.

He cocked his head to the side. "Do you think you both might have judged me a little too quickly?"

Her stare hardened. "I live in a warzone without allies. How much death and de-deshtruction do I need to see—*hic*—before condemning those doing nothing?"

"I didn't start the war," he reminded her succinctly. "I wanted no part of it and I still don't. Why does that make me a criminal?"

"You sit on your hands!" she hissed. "That is as good as being a part of the war."

Wow. She really *did* hate him. The knowledge left him reeling. He'd never really cared what others thought about him, but hearing her criticism wasn't leaving him in a good place. Like he'd drank all the water while someone next to him was dying of thirst.

"A pity Sheikh Idris didn't have a son you could marry," he said idly. "There wouldn't be a war then."

"Do you really think I'd consider marrying someone with Idris' genetics? I'm not that sh-tupid."

He released an unsteady breath. Did she think Rahim's genetics were any better? That she was willing to marry the man to win the conflict by brute force left a sour taste in his mouth. "What about Rahim?"

Her eyes narrowed. "What about him?"

"Do you love him?"

Her knuckles whitened as she clenched the glass. "Does it matter?"

"Of course it does." His throat thickened, his voice turning husky. "You deserve better than a loveless marriage."

"And my people deserve better than war and chaos."

"I'm not denying that," he conceded. "But is the sacrifice too much?

She narrowed her eyes. "No sacrifice is big enough to save my people and my country."

He rubbed the back of his neck beneath under his keffiyeh, his voice dropping to a whisper. "I wish I was as virtuous."

She blinked, her stare considering. "What do you mean?"

A knock sounded on the double doors, saving him from telling the truth. One of the doors was pushed open and a chef in his whites entered carrying a tray. Two more kitchen staff, dressed in black, followed him with their own trays.

"Good," Aziz said with a relieved smile. "Lunch is here."

The chef bowed his head, then put down a tray that revealed a plate with some flatbread along with a deep copper bowl filled to the rim with slow-cooked, marinated goat. The kitchen staff then put down pilaf, hummus, falafel and baklava for dessert, followed by plates and cutlery.

Zamira closed her eyes and inhaled the aromas while he thanked his servants.

After they bowed and retreated, he turned to Zamira and stated, "You're hungry."

She opened her eyes and nodded. "Famished."

"Then allow me." He piled some marinated goat onto her plate with some pilaf on the side, and she added two flatbreads along with some hummus and two falafel balls.

"Allow me," she echoed, one of her dark brows arched as she piled some food onto his plate in return.

"Thank you," he said with a smile. There was something intimate about her voluntarily serving him food.

What she couldn't know was that he planned on being a whole lot more intimate with her in the next seven days. He didn't have to tear her hymen to give her pleasure and a whole lot of orgasms.

His dick jerked and swelled, and he barely hid a groan as he sat across from her as she ate with gusto. She'd either forgotten about her earlier comment about the food being poisoned, or was too hungry to wait for him to take the first bite just to be sure.

She picked up a falafel and popped it in her mouth, sucking some herbs from the tip of her finger.

If his dick was hard before it was set like concrete now, his imagination working overtime at the picture forming in his head where she sucked the head of his dick with just as much enjoyment.

"Your chef is incredible," she enthused.

Aziz nodded, then croaked, "He is." He cleared his throat. "He makes exceptional Middle Eastern food, but he also enjoys cooking other national dishes. Most Friday nights he'll cook something from a different country for me to sample."

"You're very fortunate." She swept a hand over the spread on the table. "All this food at your fingertips." She winced. "Back at the palace we've begun rationing our food. War and famine means having excess to eat is a thing of the past."

His throat thickened, the back of his shoulders tensing. He mightn't fight in her war but it didn't mean he couldn't help in other ways. "I'm more than happy to send food and medicine to your people."

She gaped. "You are?"

He nodded. "I'm due to attend a meeting soon. I'll organize it then."

He had many charitable foundations. It wouldn't be unreasonable to set up another one, despite the conflict of interest it might cause against Sheikh Idris.

She smiled, then said quietly, "My people would appreciate your help."

"What about you?" he asked huskily. "Would *you* appreciate it?"

She narrowed her eyes, her warmth cooling fast. She no doubt thought his aid was too little too late. "Do you really think helping my people at this late stage excuses you from kidnapping me?"

He lifted his glass and swallowed some more *arak*, his gaze never once leaving hers. "Of course not. But I'm not about to make excuses for bringing you here. Not now, not ever."

"I don't expect excuses," she gritted. "Not from the man everyone calls *scorpion.*"

He shrugged. "I can't help the nickname that was assigned to me—none of us brothers can."

"So you don't sting those closest to you in order to get what you want?"

"I rarely need to. My hard work and forward planning has stood me in good stead."

She leaned forward and grabbed the *ibrik*, pouring herself some more *arak*. "Your sheer arrogance astounds me."

He exhaled long and slow. This was day one. He didn't expect miracles. But he needed for her to realize he wasn't the devil. Unfortunately, he'd run out of time to reassure her. As sheikh he had other obligations to fulfill.

He pushed his food away. "Why don't you eat your fill then relax for a few hours, perhaps read or go for a walk. I have to attend that meeting now."

Her relief was palpable. He hid a frown. He was used to women falling over themselves to please him, not look at him as though he was an insult to her eyes.

"I'm a big girl," she said with a cool smile. "I'm sure I'll find something to do."

His stomach hardened. "Just one thing...don't bother trying to escape." He pushed back his chair. "I have hidden cameras and guards at every exit point in the palace."

"Of course you do," she said tightly.

"I'd hate to have to punish you." He smiled before he bent and brushed his lips across her scalp. "See you soon, *albi*."

Chapter Six

She stared after him with her mouth open and her mind in tatters. *My heart.* That is what he'd called her...as though she was someone special to him, someone meaningful.

Impossible.

They might have met in the past but she hadn't seen him for over two years. She wasn't stupid enough to imagine he had real feelings for her. Not even Rahim loved her. He just enjoyed her company and appreciated her looks, and revered her title—so much so he was willing to marry her and end the war.

She was little more than a pawn in a man's world.

She lifted the glass to her lips for one last sip of *arak.* Behind every great man was a great woman. It'd become her catch phrase, one that reminded her to stay strong and do what she had to for her people. She mightn't ever rule Qadania, but she could most certainly be a strong influence.

She pushed to her feet as kitchen staff came to take away the empty dishes and leftovers. She smiled at them and said, "Please see to it none of this goes to waste."

One of the women looked at her with a pinched expression and said, "The food here is never wasted."

Zamira smiled and nodded. "Good to hear." As they continued cleaning off the table she wandered aimlessly through Aziz's suite of rooms, absently admiring his masculine style. A minute later she stopped at the mahogany carved doors, which led to the sitting room and the rest of the palace.

One of the kitchen staff bowed a little before following the rest of the servants as they opened the doors and marched through.

Aziz had said she could take a walk. Now was the time to test that theory.

She stepped into the sitting room and was almost tempted to make use of the room and wile away a few hours reading. She ignored the compulsion and instead continued out of the room and back into the bright mosaic corridors.

She had no idea where she was going, but exploring and learning about the palace that was Aziz's home seemed like a good idea. Better than good. Not only might she learn something about the man who'd abducted her, she might also find somewhere she could escape.

He might tell her she was only here for seven days, but that was seven days too long in her opinion. And how did she know if he even spoke the truth? She might be stuck with him for months, years!

And that's a bad thing?

She ignored a shiver of something that bordered too close to gleeful. Her stomach twisted. She might have had a crush on the man when she was younger but she knew better now. He was a good looking, selfish asshole. And she'd resist his charm if it killed her.

The *whirring* that was the wheels of a covered trolley brought her back to the present, a kitchenhand rounding the corridor ahead. A waft of what she guessed was lamb and lentil stew drifted her way and it was instinctive for her to follow. She didn't slow until two guards at a set of double doors stepped aside to allow the servant entry into the room.

The guards pushed shut the doors, but not before Zamira caught sight of a dozen or more children inside, all sitting at tables and waiting for their lunch. That there were also three beautiful women sitting at the tables with them made her stomach crunch.

Who were these children? They clearly weren't servants' kids, they wouldn't be guarded so stringently. Were the three women their mothers? Heat rose behind her eyelids. Was Aziz the children's father?

He mightn't keep a harem but it wouldn't be uncommon for someone in his position to have wives and mistresses who'd happily bear him offspring.

No, not wives. She would have heard if he'd gotten married. But it made sense he'd keep mistresses, probably even more than the three she'd seen.

She shivered, brushing her hands up and down her covered arms. It was slightly cooler in this wing of the palace, the air temperature regulated to no doubt keep the children more comfortable.

A boy laughed, followed by a little girl's giggle.

It sounded as though they were treated well. No doubt they were highly-prized if they *were* Aziz's children. One of them—an eldest son—would likely one day rule in Aziz's stead.

She spun on her heels and retraced her steps back through the blue and white mosaic tiled corridors. Sunlight splashed through skylights at regular intervals, making the already wide corridor feel more spacious, while countless single doors to what she guessed were smaller rooms kept out prying eyes.

She stopped and knocked on one. When no one answered she pushed the door open and looked inside. It was a sumptuous bedroom with a walk-in robe and its own bathroom. The walls were painted white with a feature wall behind a glossy timber bed showcasing mosaic tiles of gold and white.

She closed the door quietly. How many guestrooms did the palace have?

It was almost obscene to see such wealth and grandeur when her country was close to destitute. That he'd promised to send aid gave her a little bit of hope, her shoulders not bearing quite so much burden.

She only hoped he'd been telling the truth, she didn't think she could bear the weight of it all again otherwise.

When she finally found her way back to his wing of the palace, she didn't go any further than the sitting room. She picked up the camel book and dropped onto the nearest comfortable armchair before she flipped through the book's pages.

She'd always loved camels. That they were the ship of the desert that could make or break many of her peoples livelihoods meant she'd invested what she could into new breeding stock with stronger bloodlines.

Butch had been meant to be part of that future livestock investment. Her chest tightened, a rush of dizziness assailing her. Rahim, her future husband, had been an even bigger investment, one she might lose now thanks to Aziz. She sighed heavily, the printed pages and camel images distorting as weariness swept over her. Her lashes fluttered closed. She'd rest her eyes for just a moment...

When she next woke she was shocked to find she was back in the bedroom of her father's palace. She climbed out of bed and pushed her feet into her sandals before wrapping her abaya around her nightgown.

She made her way down the marble stairs, sniffing appreciatively as the mingled scents of a cooked breakfast floated her way. Her step quickened. The cheesy herbed flatbread aroma was unmistakable. They hadn't indulged in *manakish* for ages! She was almost as certain chickpea and bean stew was on the breakfast menu too.

She rushed toward the dining room. Rounding the stairs toward the large table with its twelve chairs, she noticed a stranger already seated. He wore a pristine white thobe and a keffiyeh with its gold agal. She slowed, her eyes going wide and her hand automatically reaching up to touch her bared head.

She'd left her favorite hijab on the end of her bed.

"Zamira," her father said with an indulgent smile, his heavily ringed fingers waving at her to approach. He sat in his usual place at the head of the table. "This is Rahim, the man I was speaking about to you just the other day."

She hid a frown. Her father hadn't done any such thing. She would have remembered Rahim even if it'd been nothing more than a passing chat with her dad.

He glanced at the other man. "Rahim, this is my daughter, Zamira."

"It's wonderful to finally meet you," Rahim said with a smooth smile and an appraising stare. He pushed respectfully to his feet. "Your pictures don't do you justice."

"Thank you. It's, ah, lovely to meet you too."

He smirked, then turned to her father. "I was hoping for a little more enthusiasm."

Before her father had a chance to answer, she blurted, "I haven't even brushed my hair let alone covered it!"

To say she was a little bewildered by their guest was an understatement. They rarely entertained these days. Her heart contracted. No doubt her father had his motivations for having Rahim here, and she'd bet introducing this man to her was high on his agenda.

"You have beautiful hair, it seems a shame to cover it up," Rahim said with a glint in his eyes.

She managed a smile as she took a seat opposite him, but she was no longer hungry, not when her stomach was tied up in knots. She waited until he sat back down before she asked, "What is this all about?"

Her father cleared his throat. "I was discussing the war here with Rahim, he was very...accommodating in wanting to end it."

She turned to Rahim. "Really? What's the catch?"

He threw his head back and laughed, his beaked nose and ruddy cheeks highlighted by his flashing teeth and a dark beard that grazed his chest. "I like her. She isn't afraid to speak what's on her mind."

She frowned. Why was he talking about her as though she wasn't there? Like only her father needed to know Rahim's thoughts. She looked at her dad. "Well?"

His smile faded ever so slightly. "Rahim is here to discuss an arranged marriage with you."

Her stomach sunk to her toes. "Do *I* get a say?"

"Do you want to win the war?" her father said gently, but with a glint of steel in his eyes.

She sucked a breath in through her teeth. Why was he making it her responsibility? Or maybe it'd been hers all along? She was, after all, the sheikha of Qadania. Her people were beginning to rely on her almost as much as they did her father. "Of course I do."

Her father nodded. "That's what I thought. With Rahim by our side we have a real opportunity to regain peace and stability. Our people are losing faith in us, but we have a chance now to restore it."

She turned back to Rahim. "What do *you* have to say? And why would you want to help us?"

Heaven only knew no one else had stepped in.

"I've got the power and the wealth, but I have no title or a woman to share it with. If we marry I get both the title and a beautiful, spirited wife. It's a win-win for us both."

She swallowed back sudden bile. Arranged marriages happened all the time in the Middle East but she'd imagined herself immune. How arrogant she'd been! Her dad had probably been pulling strings for months to take advantage of her maturing, good looks, anything for him to get a foothold against his enemy.

She couldn't look at Rahim a second longer. She just might say or do something irreparable. Instead she held her father's unyielding gaze. "You should have discussed this with me first."

He frowned. "We're discussing it now." His smile was placating. "I'm sure you'll grow to like Rahim as much as he clearly likes you."

She shook her head. "He doesn't even know me!"

"I know of you," Rahim interjected. "You're a sheikha, people gossip. I heard about your fire and your spirit even before I finally got to meet you."

"So it doesn't matter what I think about you—only what you think about me?"

"You could do worse," her father said sternly. "At least Rahim will help us defeat Sheikh Idris once and for all." He stood, his chair scraping loudly against the black and white mosaic tiles. "For now, I'll leave you two alone to get acquainted over breakfast."

Her heart sank. Was he serious? No single man had ever been given such a privilege. Her honor and integrity would be severely compromised by gossip alone if any servants happened to see her alone with Rahim. It showed just how desperate her father was to have Rahim as his future son-in-law.

But of course, as the sheikh of Qadania, her father *would* choose his people over his daughter. It didn't matter what she wanted.

Only after her father had stalked out of the dining room did Rahim lean forward and take her hand in his. Lifting it to his mouth, he pressed his thin lips to her knuckles, making her squirm. Not with passion but discomfort. If it wasn't for her part in this charade she wouldn't have even looked his way.

She likely would have snatched her hand away and swiped away any germs.

Not that he was ugly. Despite his beaked nose and ruddy cheeks, he was passably good looking. It was his eyes that frightened her. They were too cold, too indifferent.

Those same eyes held hers. "We could be good together. Just give us a chance. I'm not like those sheikhs who'll suffocate you with rules while hiding you away from everyone."

Despite her misgivings and an instinct to shrink away from him, hope sparked deep inside. Was she overthinking everything and seeing only what she wanted to see?

How she wished she had someone to discuss things with. Her mother had died giving birth to her, which meant she'd been raised by nanny after nanny—most of them westerners. No doubt her dad blamed those same nannies for her being so independent and outspoken. She'd picked up their modern traits.

She supposed her mother had been quiet and demure and knew her place, a modest sheikha who'd been her dad's perfect match. He still mourned his late wife despite his small harem. Men apparently needed sex more than they needed love. Her dad most certainly didn't seem to want to be in love again, while sex was a high priority.

"What do you say?" Rahim asked.

She withdrew her hand, though resisted wiping it on her abaya. "I have a lot to say," she admitted haughtily. "But whether anyone listens is another matter."

His laugh was rich and throaty, and perhaps the only thing she tolerated about him. "You really are a spirited one. So unusual for a sheikha." He pushed back his chair, then stood and stalked around the table toward her. Reaching for her and pulling her close, he said, "Let's see if you're as passionate in my arms as you are out of them."

When his lips sealed over hers she wasn't stimulated even a little bit, she felt...nothing. Then an image of Aziz popped into her head and she pretended he was kissing her. Her body didn't seem to care that she hated her imaginary lover, it only cared that she responded.

Rahim drew back, his cold eyes sparking with heat. "You're my perfect match." A satisfied smile filled his face. "Together, we'll be unstoppable."

She woke with a sharp gasp, her pulse pounding in her ears and her stomach clenched like a fist. The reenacted dream made her feel more shaken and upset than relieved, though everything inside of her wanted to believe Rahim had been genuine. So why now did she question his motives?

She didn't need to think it through. Aziz had made her second guess everything!

She pushed to her feet. *Ugh.* She needed some exercise, something to stop her thoughts from going round and round.

She stalked back into the master bedroom and into the walk-in closet where he'd supplied her with enough clothes to fill half his spacious hanging rails and shelves.

Though her first impression hadn't been favorable of Rahim, she'd accepted he was her people's only hope and she'd have to play her part in that by marrying him.

Now she wasn't sure if Aziz had opened her eyes or blinded her to the truth.

Chapter Seven

Aziz strode back to his wing of the palace with a smile. The meeting had gone well, better than expected, with his advisors on board with his plans to help Zamira's people.

Perhaps they'd known better than to argue. They might already have advised him against sending soldiers to help their war torn neighbors, but it would have been heartless to try and stop him from sending aid.

Thankfully, no had one had dared to mention his kidnapping the sheikha of Qadania, not even his Grand Vizier had summoned that much bravery. Aziz might be a generous and compassionate sheikh, but when he was on a mission, he was relentless and nothing or nobody could stop him.

He was only glad the usual politics and in-house squabbles had been kept to a minimum, it'd enabled him to focus on the promise he'd made to Zamira.

He stepped through his sitting room, noting the camel book that had been left on one of the cozy armchairs. His steps lightened a little more. He was glad she'd kept herself busy; it meant she'd be less inclined to stew about her plight. With any luck she'd be happy enough staying here with him for the week.

He snorted. Wishful thinking much?

What he *was* confident about was her being mad—or glad—that he'd left her alone for so long.

He pushed open the double doors and entered his private domain. Either way, he looked forward to the challenge. Perhaps he'd kiss away her tirade and make her realize there were better things to do with her time...and her mouth.

His dick stirred, his passion increasing with every step closer he got to finding her. She wasn't watching a blockbuster in his theater, like he'd expected. He searched the rest of his rooms, checking his bedroom last.

His frown deepened at the silence, at the utter emptiness of the rooms. Where the fuck was she?

Splash.

He stalked toward his tinted glass doors, opening them even as he spied Zamira swimming laps in the pool. He'd stepped out onto the balcony and was halfway down the stairs before he'd even thought things through.

The next minute he was on the ground floor courtyard pavers, his fingers making quick work taking off his thobe and keffiyeh. Stepping out of his loose cotton trousers, he strode toward the edge of the pool, then dived into its cool depths.

When he pushed his head free of the water, Zamira was hanging onto the coping of the pool, her eyes wide and her face flushed.

"What are you doing?" she asked.

He kept his limbs underwater as he propelled closer to her. "I'm swimming in my pool."

"That isn't what I meant!"

He closed in on her, then tucked his arms around her as he held onto the coping, giving her no room to move...to escape. "Then you'll have to stop being so cryptic," he murmured.

He was an inch away from pressing his entire body against her. His dick was throbbing with urgent need, his mind flickering with X-rated images of the two of them in compromising positions in the pool.

He sucked in a steadying breath, distracting himself by examining her up close and personal. She had the tiniest mole under her jaw, her long, dark lashes saturated with water droplets that looked like jewels. Her long, wet hair had darkened to midnight, her moist lips so damn kissable he wasn't sure if he could resist.

If he even wanted to resist.

He glanced down, his dick jerking right along with his heart. The peach bikini that outlined her full breasts and jutting nipples, and which just barely covered her pussy would be considered indecent by most of his people's standards. For him the bikini was perfection.

That she wore it despite her chaste upbringing made his dick harder still.

She really was an independent spirit, a woman with her own mind.

He didn't want to tame her—why spoil the part of her that attracted him so much? He adored her passionate nature. She was a wildcat, and he'd fight tooth and nail to make her his own.

With a groan he crushed her to him, his mouth possessing hers as his dick pressed against her belly. She froze for a second, then moaned before she yielded to him, her breasts flattening against his chest as her soft lips cushioned his mouth...testing his willpower to its absolute limits.

But though he'd sooner rip out his heart than break his word, it didn't mean they couldn't have some fun.

He let go of the coping with one hand, untying the back of her bikini top as she opened her mouth to his questing tongue. He explored inside, their tongues then touching and dancing even as he removed her top and threw it aside, her freed breasts making his breathing grow even more ragged.

He released her mouth to move lower, sucking the tip of one breast in his mouth and sucking, her nipple growing rigid. She tipped her head back with a gasp, giving him free access.

He gave her other breast the same attention, sucking and rolling her nipple around his mouth before flicking it with his tongue. Only when he moved back up to kiss her again did he brush his fingertips down her throat and between her breasts, before skimming over her flat stomach and pushing down the front waistband of her bikini bottom.

Parting her outer folds, he found her plump clit, strumming it until she was squirming and moaning into his mouth. His dick was straining when he pulled back and held her dewy stare. "Come for me."

She blinked, her lips parting and her eyes widening as he massaged her jewel harder and faster. Then she was shuddering against his hand, her whimpering gasps pushing his self-control beyond his limits.

It'd be so easy to push her bikini bottom aside, then line up his shaft to plunge deep inside her.

But he'd never broken a promise and he wasn't about to start now.

He pulled back reluctantly. Her face was flushed, her eyes shining like twin moons. *Damn fucking hell.* Did she have any idea how fuckable she looked right then? He needed her to leave before he did something he'd regret.

He cupped her ass with his free hand and lifted her so that she surged up and out of the water to sit on the coping. Her breasts trembled as her chest rose and fell as she took in deep breaths. "Go now," he said hoarsely. "Before I do something we'll both regret."

She didn't need to be told twice. Swinging her legs to the side, she pushed to her feet and ran to her towel. Then covering up her delectable body, she raced up the stairs and out of sight.

But not before her every dip and curve had been imprinted on his retinas.

He resisted touching his shaft and instead turned and swam the length of the pool, his legs and arms churning through the water. He'd need to do at least a hundred laps to get his libido back under control.

He had all week to feast on her pussy before she returned the favor and sucked his dick. Whether he could wait that long was a whole other matter.

Chapter Eight

Zamira ran upstairs and into the bathroom, locking the door behind her before she threw her towel onto the floor. Dragging off her bikini bottom, she stepped into the shower and turned on the taps, wilting beneath the hot water.

What had she been thinking? She hated Aziz with a passion!

She scrunched her eyes closed and tilted her face up into the water raining down on her. Perhaps her passion for Aziz was half the problem. She didn't know from one minute or the next whether she wanted to slap him or tear his clothes off.

She swiped the water from her eyes and reached for the luxury brand of shampoo and conditioner. She might as well indulge in all the extravagances while she was here. Once she was back home she wouldn't have any choice but to be frugal again.

Not that she minded. Knowing many of her people were struggling made her own problems seem petty in comparison.

A handful of minutes later she stepped out onto the mat and dried herself off. She looked out the window as she wrapped a towel around herself. The sky was beginning to darken into a deep violet, signaling the transition from late afternoon to night.

She swallowed convulsively. She'd be sharing a bed with the man who'd made her orgasm just by touching her intimately. Could she stop him if he wanted to take it a step further?

Did she want to stop it?

That her body ached for him while her mind rebelled was a push and pull that only added to her confusion. She shouldn't want him, she *didn't* want him! It was just lingering infatuation she'd yet to dispel.

That she'd just barely resisted drinking in every inch of his nude body was her problem, not his. She needed to get over the crush she'd had on him, and fast, before she made a complete fool of herself.

Pushing open the door, she walked to the closet before finding the most modest black nightdress and putting it on. Throwing an abaya over the top, she walked barefooted back into the bedroom, then stepped through the opened doors leading out onto the balcony.

Her mouth dried as her gaze followed Aziz swimming up and down the pool with relentless strokes. Would he be as relentless in bed? She put a hand to her chest. She could only imagine him driving in and out of her, his rhythm all-consuming.

She jumped as a knock sounded on the sitting room double doors. She spun away and hurried toward the doors before pulling one open. A chef in his whites stood behind a trolley, the dishes on top wafting with delicious smells. He bowed, then gestured at the covered food.

"Come in," she said awkwardly. She hadn't even thought about dinner, her mind had been too busy with other thoughts.

He smiled and pushed the trolley past her and toward the dining table.

"We'll eat outside, thank you," she said.

She'd enjoy the view.

If the chef noticed his sheikh swimming laps while the darkness gathered outside, he didn't make comment. Instead he set out the food along with some plates and cutlery, before he opened a bottle of wine and filled up two glasses.

"Thank you," she said, her stomach rumbling at the scents.

The chef nodded, then flicked a switch near the door, a downlight casting muted, soft illumination over the table.

She wasn't sure if it was the scent or the light, or a combination of the two that made Aziz suddenly stop swimming before he looked up to where she sat. When he reached for the edge and effortlessly climbed out, a shiver moved through her.

Even with the growing darkness she could see his rippling six-pack and his cock that was semi-erect and bigger than she'd even imagined when its head had been pressed against her stomach.

The chef coughed delicately behind his hand, and she gasped before she clasped his arm and said, "I am a sheikha, I have a reputation to uphold."

He nodded, then bowed again and said, "Your secret is safe with me."

She blinked. "Thank you. But that doesn't mean we're hiding anything! Quite the opposite. I'm his hostage, held here against my will."

If she'd had any hope that he might offer some way to escape then it fizzled out fast when he bowed yet again, then left her wordlessly to the sumptuous food and the naked visual of Aziz as he bent and picked up his clothes.

She gulped as he used his thobe to dry off before he pulled on loose pants. Surely he planned on dressing into another thobe?

He climbed the steps, his wet, dark hair that was a touch too long making her want to run her fingers through it. She shook away the thought when he stepped up onto the balcony. She even managed a smile before she said, "Once you're dressed I'll eat dinner out here with you."

"No need to wait." He took the seat opposite, his big body lithe and athletic. "Let's enjoy dinner while it's still hot."

She couldn't help but stare at his powerful abs, his corded arms and shoulders. He clearly wasn't a sheikh who sat idle all day. He was a working sheikh who knew how to work hard when needed.

"Do I measure up?" he asked with a smirk, his white teeth flashing under the soft light.

She picked up her glass of wine and chugged down a couple of mouthfuls. "You're...passable."

He arched a brow. "Passable?"

She shrugged, then ladled some lamb—or was it goat?—onto their plates, the tender meat enhanced by potatoes, carrots and peas. "Yes, passable."

Liar. You're so attracted to him in every way it borders on sickening.

She glanced up at him and couldn't help but ask, "What about me? Do I measure up?"

"You're everything I want in a woman," he said huskily. "You're not repressed by culture or society, you're spontaneous and direct. You're...perfect."

Pleasure surged followed by a twinge of guilt. He'd called her perfect after she'd called him passable. Did he know she'd lied? He was everything a woman could want, and not just because he was physically gorgeous and powerful. If he commanded a room thanks to his charisma, his brilliant intellect enabled him to captivate everyone in it.

A pity he'd ignored the war on the other side of his province's border.

She'd do well to remember that. She'd been so caught up in his presence she'd nearly forgotten her county's plight.

Digging into the meat, she took a bite. It was definitely goat. It was gamier and had more of a chew to it than lamb, though it'd obviously been cooked low and slow to increase its tenderness.

She picked up some flatbreads and put some pieces of meat and vegies in the middle before she folded it over and took another bit. The chef here was amazing.

Meanwhile her people were lucky if they got three meals a day.

Her stomach soured and she pushed her plate away. Looking up at him she asked, "How did your meeting go? Did you manage to secure aid for my country?"

He took a sip of his wine and nodded. "The meeting went very well, and yes, I managed to do just that. Aid will begin to arrive in your country early tomorrow. I have a crew as we speak who are gathering supplies, which will be loaded early in the morning."

"So soon?" she breathed.

"You'd rather I wait?" he asked drily.

She shook her head. "Of course not, I just thought with all the bureaucratic red tape it'd take days, if not weeks or months."

"I've never been a big believer in too many rules and regulations. My policies are kept simple and straightforward, which means things get done in a timely manner."

She hid a wince. How many times had her people complained about the never ending red tape they had to go through just to get permission to do the simplest tasks? Her father might have the best of intentions, but perhaps he could learn a thing to two about expediting the little things to make their people happy. As if the war wasn't making them miserable enough.

He cocked his head to the side. "You're not hungry?"

She almost said no. Then she remembered dinner would soon after be followed by bed and them sleeping together. Ignoring the heat scorching through her veins, she pulled her plate back and said, "Starving, actually."

Chapter Nine

Zamira touched her uncovered head self-consciously, then climbed into Aziz's huge bed as she listened to the shower running as he washed himself. She squeezed her eyes closed. She needed to fall asleep before he was done. At least then there was a chance he'd keep his hands to himself.

A shame sleep was near impossible when her stomach was full of knots and her imagination ran riot at what he'd planned for her.

His promise not to break her hymen hadn't stopped him from giving her an orgasm in the pool. If she'd succumbed to him so easily there, how was she going to resist him in his own bed?

Primal heat flushed her skin, and though her mind rebelled, her virgin body grew voracious as her hormones danced to their own tune.

The shower cut off and she swore she heard the towel swish over his body, drying his every contour like a lover's touch. At his approaching tread her breath released—she'd been holding it?—before the mattress compressed and he moved across the bed to where she lay perfectly still.

He pulled her into his arms, his front against her back. Her entire body stiffened. Heaven help her, his cock was huge! If he went against his word and put that inside her she'd be split in half, her hymen torn apart.

"Relax, Zamira, I've never forced a woman into having sex with me and I'm not about to start now."

It didn't stop her heart from jerking out of her chest or her body becoming stiff as a plank. But as the seconds marched into minutes and his breathing deepened as he drifted asleep, she wilted against him, her muscles untensing and her lashes drifting low.

It was actually rather nice to be cocooned so thoroughly. She'd never felt so safe and protected.

It was the last thought she had before she gave into the darkness crowding her mind.

She stepped through the foyer of her father's palace with a spring in her step. Not even passing one of her father's harem girls, whose overpowering lavender perfume was cringe-worthy, could dampen her spirit.

Thanks to her father's birthday, Sheikh Rami Al-Hadid and his five sons were visiting today! Though she'd only seen them infrequently over the years, she'd always been drawn to Aziz.

Perhaps because he'd treated her as an equal, not as some vapid sheikha wallflower without a viewpoint of her own. She might only be seventeen, but she wanted to make the world a better place, most especially, she wanted her people to live long and healthy lives and feel blessed to live in Qadania.

She rounded the corner toward the entertainment chamber, following the haunting sounds of a *ney*—an ancient flute—along with a smattering of laughter and many voices talking at once.

She stopped at the chamber's opulent mosaic entryway, her eyes scanning the esteemed guests until she found the Al-Hadid brothers. Aziz, Zayn, Raja, Sharif and Lyron. They were never far apart from one another. She guessed they took solace in the fact they were all in the same vote. Abandoned by their family and adopted into another.

She wondered if they secretly embraced or rejected their roles as sons of the sheikh. They were too inscrutable to read. Not even Aziz, with his friendlier demeanor, gave away any clues.

But then they were probably all guarded thanks to their past, one they likely knew very little about. Did Aziz—any of them—even know where they came from?

Perhaps it didn't matter. Their country was Turain now and if the gossip was correct, Turain would soon be divided into provinces for each of Sheikh Ahmad's sons. It was a rather ingenious way of keeping them as equals while giving undivided leadership to each region of the country.

Her eyes automatically returned to Aziz. That he was talking to Sheikh Idris, the one man in the group who was stirring up controversy with Qadania, caused her shoulders to stiffen and her lips to compress.

Did Aziz not know that Idris was a conniving asshole who'd take milk from a baby if it made him richer? Though her father was trying to keep the peace he really should have kicked the man out of their country!

She lifted her chin. It didn't mean *she* had to put up with the man! She marched forward. It was Aziz who noticed her first, his smile warm along with his eyes.

"Here's my favorite princess. What have you been up to, Zamira?"

She might have melted if it wasn't for Idris who looked at her like she was a tasty piece of meat. Ignoring Aziz, she glowered at the sheikh. "You *do* realize no one wants you here?"

She heard the gasps around the room. She'd definitely overstepped the mark by disrespecting her father's guest, despite their dubious friendship.

Idris narrowed his gaze, his moustache quivering right along with his unshaven, weak chin. "I was invited."

She managed a tight nod, her smile cracking her face. She really had gone too far this time, but she couldn't back down, not without looking like she was in the wrong when the opposite was true. "That was before you tried to manipulate my father into giving you our superior crude oil for second-rate prices."

Idris' face went an interesting shade of mottled purple when Aziz said, "This is a celebration. Let's not bring politics and finances into the mix."

"He's right, we're here to enjoy each other's company," a soft and sultry, feminine voice said from behind them.

Zamira turned as Idris' daughter, Nadia approached. The woman flicked a hand over her buttercup yellow abaya, the matching hijab somehow emphasizing her dark-kohl lined eyes as she turned her attention to Aziz, her smile lighting up her face like a star in the night sky.

"Nadia," Aziz murmured with a deferential nod of his head.

"Aziz," Nadia murmured huskily in return. She fluttered her long lashes. "It's been too long."

Zamira's chest tightened. It'd been ages since she'd last seen Aziz too! Not that Aziz probably noticed her absence when Nadia was in his face.

Idris nodded, his anger seemingly forgotten as he focused on his daughter and Aziz. "Nadia was speaking highly of you just this morning," he said with a fond smile his daughter's way. His mouth set as he turned back to Aziz. "I only hope her high regard of you isn't misplaced."

"I've never intentionally hurt a friend and I don't intend starting now."

"Friend?" Nadia repeated in a high-pitched voice.

For one single, solitary second, Zamira felt sorry for the other woman. Then Nadia sent him a bold, flirtatious smile, sparks all but zapping from her eyes before she said, "I'd like to think we're more than that."

Idris laughed. "Be warned, my *friend.* When my daughter wants something, she'll stop at nothing to get it."

Zamira didn't want to think about her rising body temperature or the squeeze of her ribs when she grabbed Aziz's arm before he had a chance to reply. Holding his dark stare, she said, "Would you mind if I stole you away for just a few minutes—in sight of everyone, of course."

Aziz raised a dark brow, his teeth bright behind his neatly trimmed beard. Though he was considered young—twenty-two—his manly attributes made him seem so much older. It wasn't just his facial hair, it was his brilliant eyes that seemed to see right through her, his hands that were calloused thanks to his outside work with camels and horses, his coiled strength that was obvious despite his thobe.

That he'd excelled at everything he'd put his mind to only added to his maturity, his knowledge and experience a combination that both fascinated and intimidated her.

"But of course," he replied smoothly.

She must have misheard the husky undercurrents in his voice. She glanced at Nadia's frozen smile. No, she hadn't misheard anything, not if she was reading Nadia's expression correctly.

"If you'll excuse us," he added politely to the father and daughter before he led Zamira to a more secluded part of the room. "It seems I owe you a very big favor," he said in a low voice.

"Oh?"

"You rescued me from a very...volatile situation."

She wasn't sure whether to be relieved or disbelieving. "Most men would be flattered at the very least to have Sheikh Idris' daughter interested in them."

"I guess I'm not like most men," he said with a smile that would have charmed the birds right out of the trees.

Not her though. She was more interested in his integrity than his charm and good looks! At least, that was what she told herself before she leaned closer and asked softly, "So *who* are you interested in then?"

It took everything she had not to bat her lashes and flirtatiously smile. If he wasn't like other men, then she most certainly wasn't like other women. She was strong and independent and didn't need a man in her life to make it complete.

Having someone like Aziz would just be a bonus...the icing on the cake.

His stare held hers. "I believe I'm looking at her."

Chapter Ten

Zamira woke like she was having an out-of-body experience. She was looking down at herself as she snuggled against Aziz—the one and same man who'd damn well kidnapped her!

But his words echoed in her ears like he'd spoken them just yesterday, making her soften against him even more.

Why couldn't things have stayed the same way between them all those years ago? She'd trusted him then, had had high expectations in him. But from the moment he'd turned his back on her country—on her!—instead of helping, he'd broken her trust and shattered her dreams, turning them into illusions.

Not even their last meeting almost two-and-a-half years ago had prepared her for this scenario.

"Good morning." His muffled voice against her back was deep with sleep and indulgence.

She stiffened, no longer relaxed against him. "Morning."

Even knowing he was awake it was hard not to succumb against his powerful heat and yield to his arms that were wrapped around her. One of his legs was even draped over her thigh, imprisoning her.

He nuzzled her neck. "Mm. You smell good. You taste good, too."

She wanted to jerk away from him, except his lips that pushed kisses along her nape were firing up her nerve endings. Electricity sizzled through her, cutting off all her willpower and any desire to escape.

She moaned, her lust intensifying. Then he sucked her flesh and her whole body jolted, her core twitching.

He lifted his head from her with a low and husky chuckle even as he ran his fingers through her hair. "I love that I alone know how beautiful your hair is. So silky soft, with streaks of burnished copper."

She shouldn't feel so special or adored from his words, but somehow she did. She gritted her teeth. He *was* the scorpion, his sting as lethal as his charm. He knew just the right words to say to make her forget about the war in her country, and his lack of interest in it.

Not even his offer of aid could possibly counteract his refusal to help fight against an enemy who seemed unbeatable.

She wasn't even sure if Rahim had enough brute force to overcome Sheikh Idris.

Rahim.

She'd all but forgotten he existed, and though she was supposed to marry him, all her focus was now centered on Aziz's skilled touch as he again kissed her nape while massaging her scalp.

This. Was. Heaven.

Not even his cock digging into the small of her back made her want to jump out of bed and get away from him. If anything, she wanted more. More of his mouth and hands on her. More of him, period.

Then he pulled back with a harsh grunt, rolling onto his back and stretching his arms over his head. "Our breakfast will be waiting."

Her breath caught at the back of her throat. He was seriously thinking about food right now? Her entire body was inflamed and aching! She spun around to face him, then repeated, "*Breakfast*?"

Yes, she was hungry, but not for *that* kind of sustenance. Her virgin body was going through an awakening, and she didn't want her education to end. That she wanted Aziz at all might make her stomach churn, but it didn't stop the itch that needed scratching.

"Breakfast *is* the most important meal of the day," he said, his eyes glinting. "I can easily forgo lunch if I'm busy, so long as I've consumed enough calories in the morning."

She closed her eyes for a second as a visual filled her mind of his head between her legs while he consumed his calories. She shuddered, her mouth dry and her core saturated.

"Are you okay?" he asked.

She forced her lashes apart only to find his nostrils flared, like a stallion aware of a mare in season. She swallowed hard. “I’m fine,” she muttered.

His grin was too close to a knowing smirk. “Good. I’ve got something to show you after breakfast.”

Tossing aside the bedcovers, he pushed to his feet and stalked to his walk-in closet, his bare ass and the muscles either side of his spine flexing with every step he took. She looked away, her face burning. She’d also glimpsed his cock, and it’d been every bit as long and thick as she’d recalled.

She cleared her throat and asked, “Do you always strut around naked in front of innocent women?”

His voice sounded far away as he dressed into the clothes he was wearing for the day. “I can’t say. I’ve never had an innocent woman in my bedroom before. But since I always sleep naked, I’m not about to cover up now.”

“Not even for the Sheikha of Qadania?”

“Especially not for the Sheikha of Qadania.”

She got out of bed and marched toward the walk-in closet, gaping at seeing him in western clothes. If he was mouthwatering in his thobe and keffiyeh, he was delectable in his casual gray pants and white cotton shirt.

“What are you wearing?”

He looked down at his clothes. “You’ve never seen me in anything but a thobe?”

She shook her head, then said, “Never.”

“Well, now you have.” He smiled. “I’ll leave you to get dressed.”

She waited until he left before she looked through the closet with all the clothes he’d supplied her. He really had planned her abduction in advance. She still didn’t completely understand why. Nothing would make her see him as anything but the bad guy. And nothing would stop her from marrying Rahim.

She'd do whatever it took to end the war and see her people happy and safe once again.

She paused after sliding aside a clothes hanger to reveal a white sundress with a sunflower applique on the front. Though it was ankle length with cap sleeves, it would be considered risqué without an abaya over the top. She touched her hair. It would be even more immodest without her hijab.

She snorted. She was no longer in Qadania. And if Aziz could wear western attire then why couldn't she?

A handful of minutes later she stood in front of the dressing room mirror in a pair of white heeled sandals and the white dress with her dark hair falling down her back.

She looked like someone else.

She looked...gorgeous.

It was an odd feeling. She'd grown up to be modest and not count on her looks. Usually when she looked in the mirror she saw the same woman looking back at her, with her hair covered up along with her body.

She exhaled slowly, doubt beginning to creep into her psyche.

She might be considered a modern sheikha, but was this outfit *too* much?

A soft whistle made her jump a little, her eyes lifting to view Aziz in the mirror as he stopped behind her. "You're stunning."

Her throat dried. "Thank you." She swallowed hard. "Wh-what are you doing here?"

"You mean in my own closet?" He smirked, then added, "I came looking for you."

"Making sure I hadn't made a run for it?" she asked mock-sweetly.

He placed his hands on her shoulders, his heated touch sending shivers through her. "You're not going anywhere, *albi*."

She shrugged free from his hold. "I'm *not* your *albi*. I'm your prisoner."

"You are," he agreed softly, but with such uncompromising resolve it took everything she had not to scream. He crossed his arms, his stare holding hers. "It's up to you though how you deal with it. You can enjoy your stay, or hate it, your fate is in your own hands."

She stiffened. Was her fate in her hands—or in his?

She'd certainly enjoyed his hands when he'd given her an orgasm.

His lips twitched, as though he'd read her mind. "I came in here to make sure you ate some breakfast before my servants clear the food away."

"Can't have your prisoner starving," she muttered sarcastically.

"No, I can't have that," he agreed, before he took hold of her hand and led her out through the bedroom and toward the dining room.

After a delicious breakfast of fried eggs, haloumi and flatbread, along with coffee flavored with cinnamon sticks and saffron, she followed Aziz through his palace, past the wing where she'd seen the children and beautiful women.

She forced a smile and asked, "Do you keep any mistresses here in your palace?"

"Any mistresses I've had are long gone," he answered. "They left here happily enough with the gifts I sent them off with."

She wanted to press him further, but she didn't want to look invested in his love life. She swallowed back any more questions as they finally came to the end of one wing of the palace, where robed guards stood in front of a single door engraved with lotus flowers and hieroglyphics. The guards stepped aside and bowed their heads deferentially as Aziz stalked forward.

He opened the door to an outside world showcasing date palms, which shaded a paved pathway, along with urns of hardy shrubbery and some abstract sculptural pieces. Though it was relatively early in the morning, heat pulsated from outside, the sunlight shimmering on the sand dunes in the distance.

"Where are we going?"

"I thought I'd show you some of the camels in my stable."

She beamed. "Really?"

He chuckled. "Yes, really." He cocked his head to one side. "I think I've just found the way to your heart."

She shook her head. "If you're looking for that, you'll find the way is through ending Qadania's war."

"There couldn't have been an easier way, could there?"

"You want easier? Then don't go kidnapping the one woman you supposedly want to impress."

He drew her away from his guards, his touch gentle and yet somehow powerful. "I just want you to think twice before marrying Rahim. He isn't the solution to your problem."

She almost stumbled as she followed him. "And he just might decide I'm soiled goods now thanks to you!"

Why didn't the idea make her seriously angry and upset? Instead relief flooded through her. Everything was beginning to unravel around this man, his beliefs becoming hers. Surely two days wasn't long enough to become brainwashed?

"I'm certain your father will have a physician examine you the moment you're home."

"Did it ever occur to you that I might not want that? Not only will it be invasive, it will be humiliating!"

"It's nothing a doctor hasn't seen before."

"My future husband should be the only one to see me like that!"

He nodded. "You're right, but I can't apologize, not when I'd kidnap you all over again."

"Your arrogance will be your undoing."

He pushed a hand over his face, then stated, "We shall see."

Chapter Eleven

Aziz followed the path he'd taken many times, but though he was proud of his palace and his province, and everything he'd achieved, a sour note threatened to negate everything that had led him to this moment.

He pushed the feeling away. He would not be deterred. He was certain Zamira was already second guessing her upcoming nuptials to Rahim. He only hoped he could change her mind completely.

Rahim was a dangerous man, some thought he was unhinged.

One thing he did know for sure, she was too good for the man. Aziz had known from a young boy growing into a man that anyone would be lucky to marry Zamira.

The path opened up in from of them, a big red and white barn coming into sight ahead. A yard surrounded the barn, and he pushed open the gate before shutting it behind them. Not that it mattered, the yard was empty of any stock, the camels choosing the air conditioned interior rather than the hot exterior.

The moment he pushed open the barn door, the air conditioning and the unique camel smell was like a slap in the face. Most of the animals were sitting down and chewing their cud, a few more standing and eating oats and pellets.

Zamira stepped further inside, her eyes glowing, her anger seemingly forgotten. "They're beautiful!"

"They are," he agreed.

The ships of the desert had enabled mankind to negotiate some of the most barren wildernesses in the world. Even now, with modern technology, many nomads used camels as a mode of transport.

Though Aziz's breeding program had protected many of the hardier bloodlines, he mostly focused on the sprinters, those camels that raced and won.

He smirked. Like Butch.

As if reading his mind, Zamira looked around and asked, "Where's Butch?"

"He's yours now."

She frowned. "What do you mean?"

"You wanted him, I sent him to your palace stables in Qadania. He's my gift to you."

She gaped. "Seriously?"

He reached out and brushed a hand along her cheek. "There is very little I wouldn't do for you."

Her eyes warmed. They just as quickly grew cold before she jerked her head away. "Except help my people win a war."

He dropped his hand back to his side. "It's not as easy as you might think."

"Then explain why it is you've left my people to rot while your people live their best lives?"

His heart cramped. Did she think it was easy for him to stand back and watch her country fall? It'd been hell. But although he hadn't fought in her war, he refused to see her in a loveless marriage just so she could correct her father's pigheadedness at selling their crude oil at a fairer price.

His spies had been right. The conflict really had affected her deeply.

He dragged a hand over the thick bristles of his jaw. "Have you forgotten that the once large country of Turain is now divided into five smaller provinces? Mukaite has less than a fifth of its original population and as sheikh to those people I cannot and will not risk bringing a war to their doorstep."

She seemed to deflate as she considered his words, her shoulders slumping. Then one of the camels approached and butted her with its head, making her gasp and then laugh a little as she turned and patted the female's muzzle.

"Well hello there, little one. Weren't you getting any attention?" she asked.

One of the camel keepers hurried over. "I'm so sorry if Kalie frightened you."

"No, no. She's lovely," Zamira said. "She didn't frighten me in the least."

The camel keeper exhaled with relief before looking at Aziz.

He nodded. "Zamira is very well acquainted with camels," he reassured. "She doesn't fear them in the least."

The camel keeper bowed as he smiled broadly. "Then unless I can be of assistance, I will leave you both alone."

It wasn't until the man headed away from them and to one of the stalls that separated a pregnant mare from the rest, that Aziz turned his full attention back to her. "Choose any one of these camels and it'll join Butch in your country."

She blinked at him. "It seems Kalie chose me. But if you think that will make up for kidnapping me—"

"I just like seeing you happy."

She shook her head. "If that was true I'd be back in my own country."

"*Are* you happy there?"

She leaned back, as though shocked by his question. "Of course I'm happy!" She huffed out an impatient breath. "Why wouldn't I be?"

"Why indeed."

"What is that supposed to mean?"

"Have you never stopped to question your father's behavior? Never asked yourself why he'd use you to right a wrong?"

Her eyes narrowed. "So my father can't marry me off to save our people but you can force me away from my home?"

Didn't she understand it was to save her from a lifetime of marital hell? That he hoped she'd also come to see him as more than an enemy didn't need an explanation. "You're here for seven days, not the rest of your life. Not unless you choose to stay."

She crossed her arms, her eyes flashing. "I'm counting down the minutes."

"Were you counting them down when I made you orgasm?" he asked roughly. She gasped, and he leaned closer and added, "When we kissed?"

"You're despicable," she hissed.

He shrugged. "Is it despicable to speak the truth?"

A part of him wished he had more time to change her mind about him, especially when he just might be pushing her farther away. But he had to open her eyes to the truth sooner rather than later—even if it hurt her to hear it.

While she silently stewed, he ushered another camel keeper over. "See to it you organize transport for Kalie. She'll be joining...Butch in Qadania."

"Butch?" the camel keeper asked.

Aziz smirked. "Sunburst Striker."

The camel keeper's eyes went wide. "You're certain you want to lose Kalie too?"

"I am."

"It's just that she's been carefully selected, her genetics some of the finest. Not even Sunburst Striker has her—"

I'm aware your devotion to my camels, but this is the last time you question me."

The other man's face paled. "Of course, Sheikh Aziz. My sincere apologies. It won't happen again."

"See that it doesn't."

Zamira shot him a dark look the moment the camel keeper hurried away. "That was a bit harsh."

"Your father wouldn't have done the same?" They both knew he'd have been far harsher. "If I don't show my authority when it counts, I won't be respected as the leader of my people."

She nodded. "I know, it's just...it's obvious he loves these camels."

"No more than you, I'm sure." He sighed heavily. "In the end, the camels are mine to keep or to sell...or give away."

She huffed out a breath. "Well, I'm not one of your camels. Don't treat me as one."

"You wouldn't be here now if I saw you as nothing more than one of my livestock."

"You want to change my mind about who I marry, not to mention make me believe you're a nice guy, but all you've done is make me realize how right I was not to trust you."

He wondered if it was more that she didn't trust herself rather than not trusting him. After all, it wasn't the first time she'd yielded to him. The last time had been almost two-and-a-half years ago. That memory was one he'd never forget.

But he wouldn't bring it up just now. Instead he growled, "What do you know about Rahim—*really* know?"

Her eyes glittered. "Other than the fact he is willing to step up to the plate and drive out the Qadania invaders?"

"Yes. Other than that!"

Her eyes narrowed. "He's a gentleman who appreciates me. He doesn't want to change me."

He resisted baring his teeth at her words. "It's a front. He's no gentleman. He'll enjoy breaking your spirit from the moment he slides a ring on your finger."

"Why do you hate him so much?" She sucked in a breath, her voice turning hoarse. "Are you trying to stop our marriage so that your friend, Sheikh Idris, doesn't lose the war?"

Aziz drew her out of the building and through the yards, his whole body vibrating with the injustice of her words. "Do you really think I'd choose Idris over you?"

"It seems that way!"

He opened the gate and ushered her through. "Then you don't know me at all."

"You're right—I don't! Not anymore. The man I used to idolize has a heart of stone."

Chapter Twelve

Zamira had to regain control of her emotions as she walked beside Aziz back through his palace. He'd gotten under her skin, became an inflammation she couldn't repress.

Her every cell buzzed with awareness in his presence, exacerbating everything appealing. His smoky amber scent with its deep sea undertones. His impressive height and the breadth of his shoulders. His rough-skinned hands and his long, blunt-ended fingers. His neatly trimmed dark beard that was stark contrast to the white flash of his teeth. His brilliant dark eyes that always seemed to see right through her.

She stiffened. Then there was his complete disregard for her people and the war that was breaking Qadania. She might find a whole lot of positives in his looks, but she'd never get past that one major flaw in his personality.

They were almost to his wing of the palace when a robed man sporting a long, gray beard on a cherub face hurried toward them.

Aziz slowed, his arm moving to encircle her waist.

She stepped away. She didn't need his protection. She didn't need anything from him!

Aziz frowned a little as he caught her up against him once more before he acknowledged the older man. "Amon." He turned to her. "Zamira, I'd like you to meet my Grand Vizier."

The older man bowed and said, "Sheikha Zamira, it's lovely to meet you. I can see why you're the talk of the province...and beyond."

She blinked. "I am?"

Amon nodded, then turned to Aziz. "It's why I'm here. Talk has reached Sheikh Idris and his daughter. They've heard about your rather unconventional...relationship with Zamira. They're in their helicopter and on their way here as we speak."

Aziz rubbed a hand over his face, his impatience clear. "Have my chefs prepare lunch and bring it to the green dining room. And send a barperson."

Amon nodded. "Of course, Sheikh Aziz. It will be done."

Aziz arched a brow. "No advice?"

Amon stroked a hand over his long, graying beard, his dark eyes glinting shrewdly. "Don't stir the hornet's nest by neglecting one woman for another."

Zamira repressed a hysterical laugh. The daughter of Idris had nothing to fear! She could have him! So why did her stomach cramp and her chest burn? It was absurd that she even cared after what he'd done...what he *hadn't* done!

That she was marrying another man was just one more reason not to get invested or involved in Aziz's love life.

"I'll take that into consideration," he murmured.

"Please do," Amon said. He rubbed the back of his neck. "The consequences could be dire."

It wasn't until the grand vizier stalked away to prepare for their 'esteemed' guests arrival that she said, "I will not sit at the same table with Idris." She lifted her chin. "Nor his daughter."

"Really? This might be your once chance to plead your case and make Idris rethink his position on the war."

"Except he's a stubborn old goat who won't listen to reason!"

"Might I suggest you speak to him about a lower crude oil price? If he is made aware of your *potential* marriage and the affect it might have on his own country and people, he just might reconsider."

Hope sparkled through her like fireflies spreading their light. "You think he might actually listen?"

"He'd be a fool not to...and he's no fool. Not when it comes to his success. He doesn't wear disappointment lightly."

She glanced down at her western dress, her thoughts scattering. "Perhaps I should change back into an abaya and hijab."

"No. Let's bring the element of surprise over to our side. We might need every advantage we can get."

If her mind was in turmoil before, it was in even more now. Her country's future might well hinge on the coming meeting with Idris and his daughter.

Then the unmistakable *thump thump thump* noise that were the rotors of an approaching helicopter grew louder, and her mind tangled with even more dark thoughts.

Aziz drew her down a corridor to their right, his voice gentle. "This way."

They seemed to be heading in the general direction of the helicopter. She guessed the green dining room had been chosen as it was the closest to the helipad.

Which meant the guests might arrive first.

But when Aziz finally led her into the green mosaic room that was the striking color of dark jade, it was empty. A large steel and marble table with eighteen high-backed chairs took up the middle of the room. A bar featuring the same marble stood at one end displaying different shaped bottles glistening under a small chandelier strung with silver baubles.

A barperson in a white buttoned-up jacket and loose white pants hurried into the room then, bowing before he stepped behind the bar and waited for their order.

"Would you like a drink?" Aziz asked.

She nodded. "Please."

"*Arak*?"

"Anything," she admitted. She needed something to steady her taut nerves.

She touched her unbound hair as he stepped toward the bar and ordered their drinks. "I really should have at least covered my hair."

"Yes, you really should have."

She spun around at the icy disdain of a woman's voice. *Nadia.*

The woman stepped into the room alone, looking regal in her soft, dove-gray abaya with embroidered leaves and flowers on one side, her keffiyeh a slightly darker gray. She swished the abaya's fabric, as though elaborating her superiority. "I guess you don't know how to set an example to your people."

Zamira's breath hissed out between her clenched teeth. The woman had the audacity to talk about setting an example while she looked on as her father destroyed Zamira's country along with its people!

Aziz returned with two drinks in his hands, his voice low. "Zamira is a guest in my house. You will treat her as such."

Nadia's nostrils flared. "A *guest*? From all accounts she isn't even here of her own free will."

"Perhaps you should ask me instead of talking about me like I'm not even here," Zamira said in mocking, too sweet voice.

"Well then, talk!" the other woman said imperiously.

Zamira narrowed her eyes. Two could play her game. "Why *would* I speak one word to the likes of you?"

Nadia stiffened, her entire body bristling. "Do you know who I am?" she asked in a low voice.

"Do you know who *I* am?" Zamira countered.

Nadia's eyes narrowed, her voice thrumming with menace. "Other than Aziz's kidnapped whore?"

Zamira had had enough. She stalked forward, pushing her finger into the other woman's chest and making her backpedal. "*I'm* the Sheikha of Qadania and *you* are my sworn enemy."

Idris stepped into the room, his thobe rustling. "What the fuck is going on?"

Zamira paused, her arm dropping back to her side.

Nadia froze. Then lifting her chin, she said, "Daddy, this woman dared to touch me!"

Zamira's laugh revealed no humor whatsoever. "And you *both* dared to ravage my country and take what isn't yours!"

Idris glowered, and said in a low, menacing voice "Step away from my daughter."

Aziz moved between the two women. Then giving Zamira her glass, he said, "Your drink, *albi*."

She wasn't certain whose mouth dropped open the widest between hers and his so called guests. She snapped hers closed first and accepted her refreshment with a murmured, "Thank you," before swallowing most of her drink in one big gulp.

Nadia looked too shocked to talk.

Her father had no such hesitation. He held Aziz's stare and swung a hand toward Zamira. "You have feelings for this girl?"

Aziz cocked a dark brow. "How could I not? She's everything I want in a woman."

Zamira almost preened before she remembered why she was here. "I'm sure my fiancé would agree." She forced a smile, feeling a little heady now from the drink and Aziz's praise. A pity her impending marriage to Rahim cast a sour note on it all. But this wasn't about her, it was about her country, her people. "Once we're married he's going to expel any enemies from Qadania. Together we'll end this war."

Sheikh Idris stared at her with hard, assessing eyes. "Who is this man you're marrying? Does he not care you're shacked up with another man?"

She lifted her chin, her face tingling and her eyes burning. "Rahim Mohamed will know I'm an innocent."

"Innocent?" Nadia seemed to have found her voice. "*Pah*! You're a—"

"Nadia, enough!" her father interjected roughly. He narrowed his eyes at Zamira. "When is this marriage happening?"

"No doubt as soon as I return home."

Aziz stiffened beside her, but stayed silent as he drained his drink dry.

Idris stared at Aziz, his gaze contemplative.

Nadia's lips thinned before she looked at her father. "You can't honestly believe her future husband has the capability to defeat us?"

He crossed his arms. "Rahim isn't to be discounted. He's powerful in his own right and has a lot of formidable allies. He's also a very disturbed man who kills without regard." He sent Zamira a wry smile. "Good luck with being his wife, you're going to need it."

She pushed aside the nausea swirling in her gut. Idris was just trying to intimidate her. Or was his warning something to be heeded? Though Rahim had put on a good front, what might he do to her once they were married? Despite reassuring her otherwise, *would* he be dominant and controlling?

"Sounds like they deserve one another," Nadia said with a sniff.

"She deserves the world," Aziz said softly.

"Does she now?" Idris murmured.

Zamira blinked at Aziz. Was that what he wanted to offer her? Or was he actually trying to stir the hornets' nest and saying the opposite to what his grand vizier had advised? Her stomach cramped. Was he trying to make the other woman jealous?

Nadia shook her head. "You're in love with *her*? Another man's future wife?"

Zamira looked at Aziz, as invested in his answer as Nadia appeared to be. At his closed-off expression she realized how naïve and silly she'd been. Of course he wasn't in love with her! He was determined to stop her marriage, nothing more.

The question was—why?

It led her down the same rabbit hole. He didn't want Rahim to fight for her country. She was so convinced of it now hurt and rage shimmered through her. She really had been naïve to trust him.

She sucked down the last of her drink, then muttered, "The only thing Aziz loves is doing right be his people."

"A sign of a great leader," Idris said in an approving voice.

A frown furrowed Aziz's brow. "Zamira cares very much for her people, too. So much so, she's willing to negotiate crude oil prices."

Idris snorted. "Too little, too late for that."

"That will change when I marry Rahim," she retorted.

"Not if we stop you from returning to Qadania," Nadia said with a sly smile.

Aziz put an arm around Zamira. "She is under my protection here. Anyone who threatens or touches her will answer to me."

Nadia's eyes narrowed. "Really? And what would that answer be?"

"It would be war—with or without my father's contract."

"You can't go against your father's word!" Idris stated coldly.

"I'd rather not, but I will, if I'm given no other choice."

Zamira stared at him, forgetting for a moment that her enemies were in the same room. Forgetting that he was only saying what he wanted them to hear. "You really mean that, don't you?"

He nodded, his voice wrapping around her like a caress. "I do."

That it sounded like a wedding vow shouldn't mean the world to her, but somehow it did...it really, really did.

Idris directed a flinty stare Aziz's way. "It's to your detriment your head has been turned by the wrong woman."

Chapter Thirteen

It took all of Aziz's resolve not to physically hurt the older man and deliver a message he'd never soon forget. Instead he delivered the truth. "The *wrong* woman?" He chuckled darkly. "Oh, please, Zamira couldn't be more right for me if she tried."

One of the kitchen staff entered the green dining room pushing a trolley, interrupting anymore talk. That he brought more food than what any of them could possibly eat while half of Zamira's people were on the verge of starvation would probably be a stark reminder of what Idris had taken away from her.

Idris shook his head. "And yet she is marrying someone else."

She clenched her hands into fists. "No thanks to you!"

Idris tapped his chin with a hand. "I might have reconsidered if you'd had something to sway me."

The kitchen worker had transferred the food to the table, parked the trolley next to the bar, then left the room before Zamira asked in a shrill voice, "Isn't peace and good relations with your neighbors enough?"

The older sheikh shook his head, his eyes locking with Aziz's. "We need something far more concrete than that."

Aziz's gut contracted. He should have expected this, should have known they'd have the audacity to twist things in their favor. "Let's not waste all this food," he said.

"I've heard very little goes to waste in your palace," Idris said, his voice more of an accusation than it was approval.

Nadia arched a brow. "You're not the only one with spies, Aziz."

Of course they'd know about his charity work that helped those they were hurting the most. The innocent children.

Nadia rolled her eyes and tossed her head. "I'm not hungry anymore."

Idris smiled like a crocodile. "Neither am I." He nodded at Aziz. "You know our terms. You have until tomorrow to make your decision."

"Wait." Zamira blinked. "So you're not agreeable to lowering crude oil prices?"

Idris shrugged. "I said I *might* reconsider. But I think it benefits everyone, including you, Zamira, for me to negotiate a deal with Aziz." His gaze returned to the other man. "Now that I know your Achilles heel, I can ensure my country's future once and for all."

Nadia stepped closer to Aziz, reaching up to touch his jaw and smiling like a Cheshire cat. "We can all be happy, Aziz."

Zamira turned away, her lip curling.

Aziz stepped back from Nadia. She might dress modestly but she acted totally immodest. That her father approved of his daughter's blatant lack of decorum was further proof of Idris' true colors.

"We'll be in touch," the older sheikh said with a satisfied smile.

"Bye for now," Nadia said with a fluttering of her fingers toward Aziz, blatantly ignored Zamira as she followed her father out the door.

"Are you all right?" Aziz asked, his voice strained.

"I-I don't know. What was Idris talking about? What do they want from you?"

He expelled a tight breath as he led her toward the table. If Zamira didn't want to see the truth then he wasn't about to enlighten her. And he'd rather not talk about being backed into a corner with no way out. "Let's just say it's nothing they haven't asked from me before."

She curled her hands around the back of a dining chair. "I'm not really hungry, either."

He nodded. "Yeah, me neither."

The barperson approached. "Would it please you if I took the food to the children?"

He nodded. "Yes, thank you."

Zamira looked at him. "The children?"

He nodded. "I could explain, but perhaps it is better to show you."

As the barperson loaded the trolley with food, Aziz led Zamira down a number of corridors before finally approaching a door guarded by two of his men. They bowed respectfully and stepped aside, Zamira then following him into the large dining room.

She looked around, clearly surprised to find the tables and chairs empty.

"It's a little early yet for their lunch," he said.

"Who are the children that live here?"

"They're Qadania orphans. We've taken in children who have no place left to go."

Chapter Fourteen

Her breath caught in her throat, a chunk of her heart softening. He *was* doing something for her people, after all. He'd been working behind the scenes to save the most vulnerable.

It made sense now why Idris hadn't been happy with Aziz—he knew Aziz had been helping her people.

She cleared her suddenly thick throat. "And the women here?"

"They're widowers and single mothers."

Her vision blurred. "I had no idea."

Before he had a chance to answer a stampede of feet sounded and children rushed into the dining room. She barely noticed the barperson pushing in the trolley of food from the other doorway where guards stood, not when she was surrounded with boys and girls, and mothers carrying babies on their hips.

Many of them bowed and thanked her for looking after them. She was too overwhelmed to admit it'd been all Aziz's idea and she was only now learning the truth, her mind buzzing with this newfound reality.

Within minutes she and Aziz sat at the table, everyone following suit and taking a chair. Staff appeared then and set down plates and cutlery, before portioning out the food between the children and mothers. Going by the loud *oohs* and *ahhs,* the children were obviously thrilled by what they were about to eat.

Nothing could be heard but the clinking of cutlery on plates, and within another handful of minutes, everything was devoured, not even a crumb left to be seen.

Aziz sent her a bemused smile. "I hope you really weren't hungry?"

She shook her head. "I'd much prefer watching everyone here eat their fill." She shuddered. "To think this was going to feed Idris and Nadia. These women and children appreciated it so much more."

He nodded. "These are just some of those who need help. I only hope my aid has helped many more."

"I'm certain it has," she said softly, her chest warming and her pulse accelerating just by being near him and knowing he was a far better person than she'd given him credit for.

So why did he look so...sad?

It was the only emotion she could clearly lock onto. Was it because she'd failed to negotiate with Idris to end the war? Or was it because Idris was manipulating Aziz?

Her stomach crunched. Idris surely wasn't dragging Aziz into fighting the war against her, was he?

The possibility almost made her ill.

Then she looked around at her people that he'd saved and she knew she was wrong. He wouldn't be trying to save the very people he'd have to attack.

A young woman with a baby on her lap smiled at Zamira. "We are so grateful to know you are here for us, Sheikha Zamira. Your boyfriend has been very kind to keep us here until it's safe to return home."

Zamira shook her head. "Aziz isn't my—"

"We're only too happy to help," Aziz interjected.

The baby started crying then and the young mother jiggled him even as the toddler in the chair next to her pulled at her abaya, wanting attention.

"Allow me." Zamira pushed to her feet and held out her hands for the baby.

"You're sure?" the young mother asked, relief filling her face.

"Of course I'm sure." She drew the baby into her arms, then sat back down while she crooned at him, making his cries disappear and his eyes widen as he watched her.

"You're a very special little boy," she said, smiling down at him. When he smiled back up at her, his mother gaped.

"You're so good with him, he doesn't trust anyone easily." She kissed the top of her toddler's head, then added, "You'll make a wonderful mother someday."

Zamira smiled, though her stomach lurched at the thought of having a baby with Rahim. She really didn't want to have his children.

And yet you're willing to marry him?

The woman glanced at Aziz. "Together you'll make beautiful sons and daughters."

Zamira didn't even try to protest this time. It was easier to just go with the flow and enjoy the moment as she lingered with the mothers and children. Though many of them had been through hell and back losing their homes and families, they were optimistic about their future, hope bright in their stares as they looked to Aziz and then Zamira and back again.

It should have made her uncomfortable. Instead she was beginning to yearn for that same outcome herself, the spark of longing inside threatening to burst into an all-consuming wildfire.

When she finally handed back the baby, her arms were aching along with her heart. She was committed to do right by her people and she'd do everything possible to make that happen.

Yet it didn't feel wrong when Aziz reached for her hand as they walked back to his wing of the palace. Nothing could have felt more right. She smiled up at him, admiring his profile, his height and commanding presence.

She felt his eyes on her a whole lot more as they traversed the corridors that were a beautiful mosaic blue and white pattern, a work of art.

They entered his suite of rooms, but it wasn't until they stepped into the kitchen that they noticed a platter of fruit and nuts and had been left on the island counter.

"Your servants look after you," she said with a smile.

He nodded. "They noted we didn't eat." He picked up a bunch of dark grapes, then plucked one free and held it to her mouth. "Try one," he said huskily.

She opened her mouth and he popped it inside, his fingertips brushing her bottom lip and making her nerve endings tingle. Then she bit into the fruit, its tangy sweetness filling her mouth.

"Good?" he asked, his eyes that held hers shimmering with heat.

"So good."

How did accepting a grape from his hand make her whole body come alive? She trembled with anticipation, leaning toward him even before he popped the next grape into her mouth. Except this time she closed her mouth on his fingertip and sucked.

His groan sent shivers down her spine while heat flushed her skin.

All the heated looks, the awareness and tension since their moment in the pool—and beforehand—had coalesced into this moment.

He withdrew his finger from her mouth and said huskily, "You have some juice on the corner of your mouth." When she went to wipe it away, he clasped her hand and said, "No, allow me."

But instead of brushing the juice away with his thumb, his head swooped low and he kissed it away. Their gazes locking, he groaned and kissed her fully on the lips.

She closed her eyes and surrendered to their chemistry, the electricity that danced through her taking her to another place entirely, somewhere passion and high intensity emotion belonged, and where war and sadness didn't exist.

Their mouths were locked when he drew her closer still, his arousal pressing against her stomach. Then he spun her around and lifted her until she was sitting on the bench next to the fruit platter.

He peeled his mouth away from hers, his burning stare holding hers. He didn't ask for permission, he didn't need to. She was desperate for him to relieve the ache within, an urgency that demanded he show her the way.

He pulled her dress up and she wiggled one way then the other so that the fabric didn't get stuck under her. She lifted her arms as he drew the dress up and over her head. Tossing it aside, his breath hissed as he took his fill of her, drinking in her body that was now clad in nothing more than white lacy panties and a matching bra.

"I need these off, right now," he said in a low, authoritative voice.

She didn't resist, she *couldn't* resist. She lifted her ass up as he peeled her panties down her legs, then threw the scrap of lacy fabric aside, baring her most intimate part to his heated stare.

"Fucking glorious," he breathed. Snaking his arms around her back, he unclipped her bra, her breasts falling free. He drew her bra free with a reverent sigh, then stepped back to take a long, slow look at her. "I'm never going to get enough of you."

Though it was forbidden in her culture to be exposed in any way in front of a man who wasn't a husband, there was something natural and liberating about being nude in front of him. She wanted him to like what he saw—and he most definitely did!—she wanted his approval in every way.

Then he bent low, and he covered her nipple with his mouth and sucked gently before flicking it with his tongue.

She jerked and moaned, more electricity pulsing through her nerve endings to build deep inside her womb. He scraped his teeth along her hardening nipple and she jerked yet again before he kissed away the sting. By the time he'd done the same to her other breast, she was leaning back on her outspread hands and quivering with red-hot need.

She was turning to jelly when he kissed his way down her front, sticking his tongue into her navel and swirling it around, as though giving her a sample of what was to come. Then he was kissing his way to her core, her legs opening for him even before he'd thumbed aside her outer lips. "I'm going to make you come so hard for me," he said hoarsely.

He closed his mouth over her clit and rolled the jewel around with his tongue, the jolt of fire that shot through her making her body flood with preparation for his entry. She squeezed her eyes closed, frustration filling her knowing he wouldn't break his promise. Her hymen would stay intact.

Then he sucked on bundle of nerves and she was lost...completely, utterly lost, her mind shutting down as her body imploded and sent her into a spinning vortex made up of rushing stars with bursts of brilliant colors.

He stuck the tip of tongue inside her and swirled it around her inner flesh. She jolted and cried out his name as though he'd branded his initials into her flesh.

Perhaps he had.

She shuddered as aftershocks of pleasure raced through her.

He mightn't know it, but she was his now.

She couldn't marry Rahim.

Chapter Fifteen

Aziz hadn't ever been so close to losing control after being instrumental to making Zamira lose hers. But even with his dick inflated to the point of pain and throbbing like it was on fire, he sensed a change in her. A pity he wasn't sure exactly what that was other than her having to admit to herself she couldn't get enough of him.

She shuddered beneath his mouth, her core saturated and receptive now to so much more from him. He lapped at her pussy, drinking in her essence and flicking her sensitized, swollen bud with his tongue to make her gasp and jerk all over again. His lungs expanded as satisfaction filled him. He loved plundering her willing body.

She'd make someone a very happy husband.

His breath as quickly escaped.

Rahim didn't deserve her.

Dragging his tongue one last time along her seam and around her plump clit, he kissed his way back up her body before reclaiming her mouth. He pushed his tongue deep between her lips, wanting her to taste what he'd done to her.

Wanting her to remember how he'd claimed her in every way but how it counted.

When he finally pulled back, his eyes taking in her mussed hair, her kiss-swollen lips and her dazed, slumberous stare, he croaked out, "Promise me you won't marry Rahim."

Her lashes fluttered. "I don't—"

"You can't," he cut in savagely. "Not now. Not ever." When she winced he realized he'd squeezed her upper arms. He released her. "I can stop your war without you having to marry that man," he said in a gentler tone that still spoke volumes.

She blinked. "You can?"

He nodded. "I swear on my life."

She smiled at him, all dewy-eyed and soft. "I believe you. And...I don't want to be with Rahim anymore. I *can't* be with him."

His eyes slid closed for a second as every cell in his body slumped with relief. "You don't know how happy that makes me."

"I'm glad you feel that way," she said huskily.

She pushed off the island counter, her gorgeous breasts jiggling as she landed on her feet in front of him. She licked her bottom lip, but there was a determined glint in her eyes when she said, "It's my turn to pleasure you."

His breath cut off somewhere deep in his throat. "You don't need to repay me—"

"I *want* to take you in my mouth. I want you to lose control like I did."

He wasn't about to argue. He kept his arms to his sides as she crouched low and undid his pants. She pulled them down along with his boxer briefs, and as he stepped out of them, his dick was so full-to-bursting even the scrape of the fabric and the touch of air on his shaft seemed magnified a thousand times over.

Holy shit. One touch from her silken mouth and hands and he just might explode. He couldn't have that. He wanted to savor—

He jerked with a low growl as she opened her mouth and drew him into her mouth, her moist lips suctioning him while her tongue cushioned his shaft. He reached for her head, pushing his fingers through her hair with enough pressure to encourage her to take him a little deeper.

She didn't disappoint.

She was a natural.

Had he ever enjoyed oral more? He groaned as she sucked him up and down with ever increasing movements. Definitely not. His legs almost buckled as she rendered him powerless. Despite her innocence, or perhaps because of it, she was taking him to a whole higher level of pleasure and delight.

He wouldn't just stop her war, he'd totally give the world to her if he could!

Then the head of his dick hit the back of her throat and he knew he was gone. His balls lifted and ecstasy burned through his veins, his seed exploding into her mouth. That she didn't gag was a credit to her. That she swallowed it all was an even bigger surprise that amplified his delight.

He gentled his grip on her hair, stroking gently even as she released him and looked up at him with big, shining eyes. "How did I do?"

"Baby, you were perfect."

He released her hair and reached for her hands. When she accepted his grip he drew her onto her feet, then bent to kiss her with tender restraint. It wasn't until they broke apart that he said, "I only wish you could stay with me forever."

Chapter Sixteen

Zamira lay awake next to Aziz as he slept soundly. Though she was exhausted, her mind went over everything that had recently happened, most especially what Aziz had said to her after she'd taken him in her mouth.

I only wish you could stay with me forever.

What exactly had he meant by that? Didn't he realize she'd accepted he was a part of her future...a big part? She'd already said she wouldn't marry Rahim.

Aziz muttered something in his sleep, then pulled her even closer against him. She smiled, her lashes fluttering closed. She was safe and secure in his arms.

She had to stop overthinking everything.

With a little yawn, she finally allowed sleep to take her.

Zamira stepped out of a strange fog and into a room crowded with people who were drinking and laughing.

She frowned, staring at her surroundings as a memory niggled. She'd been here before. She looked down at her midnight blue abaya that was embroidered with a spray of diamonds that looked like stars in the night sky, her silver hijab emphasizing the embroidery. She'd worn this before, too.

The thought no sooner formed before it dissolved and she became entrenched in the moment. She spied her father talking to one of his advisors along with Sharif on one side of the room, and she automatically scanned the remainder of the room for the rest of Shari's brothers, explicitly Aziz.

The hairs on the back of her neck prickled a second before her gaze found and then met his. Though he was in a group of people who were talking animatedly, he didn't appear to notice, his focus was all on her.

She smiled, her face warming. On the few occasions they saw each other, he always made her feel special, like she was worth his attention.

It was a unique feeling. As the daughter of a sheikh it often seemed like she was invisible while her father took center stage.

She drifted forward even as Aziz moved toward her until they both met somewhere in the middle of the room. Everyone and everything seemed to disappear as they reunited.

"Zamira," he said huskily. "I was hoping to see you."

"Where else would I be?'

He grinned and nodded. "It *is* your home," he conceded.

Someone nearby laughed raucously. They'd clearly had too much wine or *arak*. Likely both.

He winced. "Do you want to find someplace a little quieter?"

"Good idea."

They wandered through the crowd, his hand a perfunctory touch on the small of her back as he guided her. She noted one of his brothers, Raja, watching them leave with his usual watchful gaze. He never seemed to miss a thing. But then, she supposed he hadn't been called Falcon for nothing.

Then they were stepping outside to where fairy lights were strung overhead along the portico ceiling and in the tree branches and shrubbery. It gave the gardens a magical, surreal touch as they walked down one of its many pathways to where a fountain sprayed water in the middle of a pond.

He drew her to where the shadows of a grouping of date palms concealed them, then reaching out, he clasped her shoulders, his hands warm even through the fabric of her abaya. "I've been waiting for so long to get you alone," he said huskily.

Her heart stuttered, a seed of yearning sprouting inside, its tendrils quickly growing. "Really?"

"You doubt it?" he asked, his voice a low growl.

"Last time we spoke, a little over a year ago, you told me you were looking at the woman—*me*—you were interested in. Then I heard nothing from you again!"

"You were too young," he said roughly. "Not even eighteen."

She lifted her chin, fire in her belly making her ask, "Then what's your excuse now I've come of age?"

"Do I need an excuse to kiss you?" he asked.

He didn't give her a chance to answer. With something between a growl and a groan he swooped low and claimed her mouth with his own, his lips dominant and yet somehow tender.

She froze for a second, her nerve endings firing between shocked hesitation and stark passion. The latter won out. She relaxed into his arms and kissed him back, made heady by his ardor and his obvious skill. Damn, she'd never realized kissing could be so intoxicating...so right! It was like riding a dizzying rollercoaster and—

Someone cleared their throat. Her thoughts froze even as she jerked from Aziz's arms and spun around panting, her senses reeling as she faced Raja.

He cocked a brow, his dark olive skin giving him a shadowy, rakish appearance. "I'm sorry to interrupt such an intimate moment, but I thought it prudent of me to let you know the guests have noticed you both missing. If you leave now you just might stop further gossip from spreading."

Aziz stiffened. "If you think we care what some nosy—"

"You mightn't care, but I'm sure Zamira does," Raja interjected. "As the Sheikha of Qadania, her reputation means everything if she is to secure a decent, future husband."

Aziz's hands fisted. "I think you misunderstand the situation. I—"

"Raja is right," she said in a shaky voice. "I'm supposed to be a role model to my people. I'm disappointed in myself."

"You did nothing wrong," Aziz said in a quiet, yet forceful voice.

"Perhaps not in your eyes," she rebuked before she stepped away from him and toward his brother. "But others won't see it that way."

It wasn't until she'd swept past Raja and back toward the party that she realized how empty and desolate she felt inside.

She'd never been kissed before, never even been touched romantically by a man. Now that she knew what it felt like, she wondered if she'd crave it forever more, though heaven help her if Aziz was the only man who could sate her newfound hunger.

Zamira woke, instantly aware she was in bed alone while simultaneously sensing Aziz's eyes on her. Her lashes fluttered apart and she looked up at him standing beside the bed. Goosebumps rippled over her skin. He was drinking her in as though he'd stumbled in from the desert.

"Good morning," she croaked.

"Morning," he answered. That he'd left out the 'good' seemed significant somehow.

She blinked. "Is breakfast waiting?"

He shook his head. "No. That isn't waiting."

"Then what is?"

Something pained crossed over his face, like he was physically hurting. Then a mask slid over his expression, blocking out every nuance and thought as he said, "Your father is here."

"What?"

He scrubbed a hand over his face. "Your father is waiting to take you home."

Shock for a moment rendered her speechless. All she could get out was, "But my seven days here aren't up yet?"

"I'm not holding you to that, not anymore," he said hoarsely. "You're free to go."

What the hell was with the hurt that ripped open her heart and poured blood into her soul? "You *want* me to go?" she asked, her voice breaking right along with the trust she'd finally given him.

His stare darkened. "It doesn't matter what I want."

What did he mean by that? It was what *he'd* wanted that had seen her kidnapped and forced into captivity in the first place!

She deflated suddenly. "I understand. I'm not marrying Rahim now, so you've got what you wanted. Now you can cast me aside like yesterday's news."

"That's not true," he growled. He blew out a harsh breath and shook his head, becoming distant. "It doesn't matter anymore."

It doesn't matter?

His words were like multiple spears through the heart. Of course it mattered! At least, it did to her. That it didn't matter to him was more than obvious now. That she should be dancing on the rooftops and shouting with glee meant little right then. This might be what she thought she'd wanted, but she realized now that somewhere along the way it'd become the last thing she needed.

She flipped the bedcovers aside and swung out of bed. "Then I guess I'd better get out of here."

She'd clearly overstayed her welcome.

She pushed to her feet and went to move past him. He clapped a hand on her upper arm. "Just know one thing...you'll always be my *albi*."

My heart.

Words clogged in her throat and she froze for a second before wrenching her arm free. "My heart belongs to no man."

Not anymore.

Chapter Seventeen

By the time Zamira had dressed into a wispy, fern-green abaya with a matching hijab and flat shoes, Aziz had gone.

She swallowed back hiccupping tears. It was for the best. He'd ruined her life enough. Her being kidnapped would be the talk of her country, the speculation alone ruining her for any future marriage.

Not that she cared about Rahim anymore. Even without her promise to Aziz, she knew with absolute certainty she could no longer marry Rahim. That she'd once promised herself that nothing would stop her from marrying the man made her nauseous and had her question her sanity.

She must have been mad! Not even her own people would have expected that big a sacrifice from her.

She only hoped Aziz would keep his word and stop the war.

Of course he would. If he was nothing else, he was honorable.

With a little sniffle, she took one last look at the bedroom with its too many memories, then stalked out of it and through the sitting room before she stepped into the corridor. A young servant, a boy who was probably no older than twelve, stood waiting for her, then bowed a little before he gestured for her to follow him.

She was growing numb by the time he led her through a maze of corridors to a room with glass doors that were made hazy by its colorful stained glass depicting the golden sun setting behind green-gold mountains. The boy stopped, then bowed once again, before gesturing her toward the doors.

She murmured thanks, then waited until he'd disappeared back down the corridor before she approached the room. At hearing voices behind the doors, she slowed, her ears straining.

She heard her father's rumbling voice first.

"There was a time I'd hoped you'd marry my daughter, before your father—my supposed good friend—betrayed me. It's a real shame it's come to this."

"I had hoped for the same thing." Aziz's voice was flat, emotionless. "But my people are peaceful. I cannot risk a war by marrying the wrong woman."

The *wrong* woman? Tears pricked her eyes and rage filled her heart. She'd been right the first time. The only thing he truly cared about was his people.

He certainly didn't care about her.

That he'd called her *albi*—my heart—had been a big fat lie.

She shoved open the doors and stomped into what appeared to be a library. But she wasn't taking notice of the new and aged books on the shelves, or the groupings of armchairs that gave a warm, ambient vibe—if only Aziz and her father weren't sitting in two of them like they were long, lost friends!

Her distorted, red-misted stare focused on Aziz. "You selfish, egotistical bastard!" she hissed. "What man kidnaps a woman, then sends her packing as though she's excess baggage—no!—disposable garbage!"

He pushed to his feet. "You're going home because you're a precious jewel," he corrected softly. He stalked toward her, leaving her father in his chair as he approached. "You're too good for Rahim, and you're too good for me."

She blinked at him, her coiled muscles making her feel like a deer ready to bolt. "What? That makes no sense whatsoever!"

Her father abandoned his armchair to join them. "Aziz has agreed to marry Nadia."

Icy rejection rushed through her, freezing her in place. Yet a feather could have knocked her over thanks to the weakness flooding her limbs. She shook her head. The signs had all been there, staring her in the face, but she'd been in denial, too preoccupied by her growing feelings for Aziz to see the truth.

"And in return," her father added, his gaze taking in her reaction, "Idris will withdraw his troops from our land and our crude oil supplies."

She was too dazed, too damn wounded to be thankful. She stared at Aziz, her voice cracking. "You *want* to marry Nadia?"

"It will set you free."

"And bind you to a lifetime of matrimony!" she stated bitterly. "You don't love her."

He looked away, his lips twisting. "No, I don't."

Her father stepped forward, his hand curling around her arm. "Come, Zamira. Nothing you do or say now will change anything. Just be glad the war will finally end."

"And Rahim?" she croaked. Not that she cared about him one bit, but she needed to know she really was free once and for all.

If she couldn't have Aziz, she didn't want anyone.

"He's furious," her father acknowledged drily. "But he knows better than to face down two powerful allies now."

She glanced at Aziz, wishing things could have been different. Her heart wrenched and she blinked back bitter tears. Would this be the last time she'd see him? "Then I guess this really is goodbye."

His lips flattened and his eyes flashed, as though doing what was right by his people rebelled against doing what was right by him. "Until we meet again," he said hoarsely.

He reached for her hand and kissed the back of her knuckles, turning her hand around then and kissing her palm. Tingles of electricity danced through her even before he closed her hand into a fist and held it against his chest. "Goodbye, my heart."

She didn't have then energy to counter his words. It took everything she had just to jerk free of his hold. Her chin high, she walked through Aziz's palace with her dad, before taking the stairs up onto the roof's helipad, where she climbed aboard the big metal bird that would take her home.

Home? Just where was that now, exactly?

She watched with empty eyes as the rotors increased with speed and the pilot maneuvered the helicopter into the air. The huge white rooftop beneath along with the lake, which glistened at the front of the palace like a beautiful oasis, grew smaller and smaller as they lifted, the desert growing larger.

Then they swung away and the palace and lake became a speck...then nothing.

Chapter Eighteen

Aziz lowered his chopper onto the helipad in the backyard of Sheikh Idris' city palace. Despite the buildings surrounding the palace below the grassy knoll it sat on, there was still plenty of sand to swirl up into the air before settling once again as the rotors slowed.

He took off his aviation headset with a weary sigh. He rarely piloted his own helicopter, but he'd needed some alone time. A pity it hadn't stopped him from thinking about Zamira. Not that he was surprised. Since she'd left a little over a week ago she had been the center of his thoughts.

That he ached to be with her wasn't something he could do anything about, despite the fact he loved her...had always loved her.

It was why he was committing himself to another woman. Zamira wanted to stop the war. Marrying Nadia was the only way he could guarantee that would happen without involving his people in a long and bloody conflict.

He stepped out of metal bird and automatically ducked low as he pushed on sunglasses to protect his eyes from any lingering sand. It wasn't until he followed a paved pathway that he spotted Nadia waiting for him.

He almost flinched, then forced a smile in greeting as he approached, though a sour taste filled his mouth as she beamed right back at him.

Though it was unfair of him to marry her, it wasn't as if she didn't know how he felt about Zamira. Nadia clearly didn't care that he was in love with the other woman, she only cared that she got the man she wanted.

She held out her hand. "I'm so glad you could come today."

He took her hand dutifully in his, quickly aware of a nearby photographer snapping pictures at the distinct sound of its constantly clicking shutter.

She smiled. "Don't mind my photographer. He's here to take pictures as proof of our reunion."

He resisted dropping her hand like a hot potato. "Reunion?" he repeated.

She flushed a little. "That's what I'm calling it. We've known each other for a long time and have met on many occasions. Only recently have we realized just how good we are together."

So that was the story she'd concocted, one she'd expect him to reiterate. Sudden hostility flooded through him, but he kept his voice light when he asked, "Is that story really necessary?"

"Of course it is. How else should we get the word out that we're dating and soon to be married?"

"A public announcement isn't enough?" he asked drily.

"Oh, you're such a man!" she said. Then standing up on tiptoe, she pressed her lips against his in a brazen display for a woman in her position. A whole lot more clicks sounded as the photographer got in shot after shot, Aziz making himself respond even though he wished it was Zamira he kissed. Zamira he held in his arms.

He pulled away first, all too aware of her flushed face and glittering eyes. If he wasn't turned on then she most certainly was. She was panting when she admitted, "That probably wasn't the most appropriate behavior for a sheikha, but since we're announcing our nuptials soon enough I can't see the harm."

She wrapped her fingers more securely around his hand. "I've planned a lovely dinner tonight at my favorite restaurant. It's a very public place frequented by celebrities. I'm certain the paparazzi will be there."

He exhaled slowly. He'd expected some publicity in their...relationship, just not straight away. But of course Nadia wanted to get the ball rolling and fortify their commitment.

He forced yet another smile as he walked with her past the photographer. This was literally day one of pretending to be in love with her for the rest of his life...and he was already trying not to regret it.

*

The next four hours spent talking to Idris and his dignitaries had been nothing short of grueling. It was almost a relief to slide into the back seat of a sleek black sedan, the air conditioning cooling his heated skin and repressing a sharp need to escape, despite Nadia waiting in the car for him.

She smiled at him with her plump, ruby-red lips and her glittering, hungry dark eyes. She was clearly beyond happy with the present situation and didn't give a damn about his feelings.

"I can't wait to show you off," she said huskily, her fake lashes fluttering.

He had to admit she looked stunning in her black abaya and hijab with gold accents, her face carefully enhanced with cosmetics.

Zamira didn't need make-up, her natural beauty was more than enough.

He shook his head. He had to stop thinking about her.

He managed to engage in conversation with Nadia as their driver took them through the busy streets of the city she called home. That the palace had been built on a knoll in the middle of the city meant Idris and his daughter had the convenience of city living along with the privacy of their own space.

The driver pulled up in front of glass-fronted restaurant with beautiful lamps lighting up the steps leading to its entrance. His heart sank at seeing the paparazzi standing near the steps, waiting like vultures to take photos of any celebrities.

Nadia giggled. "What did I tell you?" She put a hand on his thigh, her fingers digging into his flesh. "We'll be the talk of the country, perhaps even the world."

He nodded stiffly as he shifted his leg away. No doubt Zamira would also hear the news soon enough. That it made his heart wrench acknowledging her hurt amplified exactly who he really cared about.

Then the driver opened their door and Aziz climbed out of the back seat, proffering Nadia his outstretched hand as she climbed out after him. Cameras flashed, assaulting his eyes. He repressed a sigh. He should be used to this kind of publicity, except in his country his privacy was respected a whole lot more.

Nadia held onto his arm as they headed toward the steps, but she slowed and then stopped as the reporters shouted out questions.

"Can you tell us how long you have been dating?"

"How serious are you two? Can we expect a wedding anytime soon?"

She smiled at the reporters and cameramen. "Sheikh Aziz and I have known one another since children, but we've only just officially started dating." She fluttered her lashes at him. "I guess you could say we're getting serious since wedding plans are already underway."

The reporters went silent before they exploded with more questions, their raucous voices hurting his head. Aziz didn't wait around to answer any of them, he climbed the steps, Nadia having little choice but to follow him or be left behind.

It wasn't until they stepped inside the restaurant, classical music softening the modern tone of its glass and steel interior that his heart rate settled. A waitress stepped out from behind a stacked-stone counter and led them to a secluded table with a shiny white tablecloth, a grouping of aromatic, flickering candles chasing away the shadows.

He drew in a steadying breath before ordering a bottle of wine and leaning back in his seat, his tense muscles slowly uncoiling.

Then Nadia held his stare and said, "I think that went well."

"Do you?" he grated.

A frown cut twin lines into her brow. "I know right now you're not overly excited about our future together, but I really believe I can make you happy—if only you'll let me in."

Impatience roared through him like a freight train. "How can you accept being second best to someone else?" Realizing how heartless that sounded, he added gently, "You could have any man you wanted."

"Except I've always wanted you," she said simply, her face staying serene and composed. She was totally unaffected by who or what he wanted. All she saw was the prize at the end—her future husband.

He pushed a hand over his face, suddenly conscious of just how flat and empty he felt inside. Was this charade even worth it? He sighed heavily. No, it wasn't. He was throwing away any chance of love to prove *what* exactly? His sacrifice wasn't making Zamira any happier, either. He'd seen the devastation in her face when she'd left with her father.

He voiced his feelings before things could get any further out of hand. "This—*us*—isn't a good idea," he admitted.

Her eyes narrowed, her serenity forgotten as her face turned a mottled purplish color. "We're getting married to end the war between my country and yours," she said, her voice sharp.

Yours? His heartbeat surged, his every cell prickling. That it hadn't been a slip of the tongue, not going by her malicious, triumphant eyes, didn't help the shock flooding his system.

She laughed, the sound grating. "Yes, Qadania is *your* country of birth. But I guess you didn't know that, did you?" Her full lips twisted into a parody of a smile. "I guess my father's spies are a whole lot better than yours at digging for answers."

He managed to keep his voice neutral when he said, "If I'd wanted to know my birthright, I would have asked my father."

"Even if you'd asked, I doubt he would have told you. Sheikh Rami wanted all of his sons to be proud Turain men, untainted by the origins of their birth."

"And that is what he got," he answered. "Regardless of our heritage, my brothers and I consider Turain our own, along with our provinces and its people."

She sniffed, her voice more cajoling as she added, "If you *truly* cared about your birthright, you wouldn't think twice about marrying me. After all, I'm willing to let slide that your mother was a whore and your father an unknown. All that matters is who you are now."

A frisson of disbelief burned through him, followed hot on its heels by incandescent fury that she dared to talk about his parents like they were shit under her sandals. "And I was willing to let slide that your father is a war criminal and you his biggest supporter."

She laughed delicately, as though completely immune to his precarious emotional state. "Relax, you're the wealthy sheikh of your very own province. People will only see what they want to see."

He inhaled roughly as he looked at her, distaste churning in his stomach. It was time she looked into her own mirror. "All I know is what I see."

She frowned. "What is that?"

"That you and I aren't so different."

Her pensive face relaxed. "I thought you were suggesting—"

"You were also born to a whore," he interjected.

She jerked back, her eyes bulging. "My mother was once my dad's favorite concubine. She was very highly regarded. She lives in a townhouse now, retired from royal life."

"It doesn't change her status," he said. "She was never royalty."

The bottle of wine arrived then, the waitress deftly opening the bottle and pouring them each a drink before quickly disappearing.

Nadia bristled as she stared at him. "You dare to offend my family!"

"You dare to offend mine?" he returned silkily.

He really had been stupid, totally crazy to face a loveless future with a woman who cared only for herself. His heart didn't belong to Nadia.

He sucked down the wine in his glass before pushing to his feet. "We were never going to work. I'm only glad I realized that before we became husband and wife."

She stood. "If you think you'll leave me to be with that sheikha bitch you've been sniffing around you have another thing coming!"

His smile was hard, merciless as he looked down at her. She shrank back, her hand trembling as she lifted her wine and gulped it down. His lip curled. For the first time in too many days he knew exactly what he had to do. "Just try and stop me."

"What do you think you're doing?" she shrieked as he pivoted and walked away. Any semblance of decorum and being a royal was stripped away from her as he continued on his way. "You can't leave me like this!"

His step didn't falter.

More camera flashes half-blinded him as he descended the steps alone.

"Where is Sheikha Nadia?" one of the reporters asked.

He stopped, giving the reporters a brief smile as he explained, "Nadia and I have decided we're better suited as friends."

One of the reporters looked animated as he asked, "There have been rumors of a certain other sheikha getting your attention. Is the gossip true?"

"I guess we'll just have to wait and see," he answered cryptically.

Though Nadia deserved his wrath, he wouldn't see her dragged over the coals thanks to a nasty public break-up.

He ignored all further questions from the paparazzi as he stalked toward the car that'd taken him and Nadia to the restaurant. The driver was surprised to see Aziz so soon, but masked his expression as Aziz said, "Please see to it the sheikha gets home safely."

The driver bowed. "And you, Sheikh Aziz?"

"I'll find my own way home." He glanced down the street lit up by streetlights, taking note of the glitzy shops. It was more than apparent the top-class restaurant wasn't the only quality store in the area. It'd be a bit silly not to take advantage of the late night shopping. "But first...there's something I have to do."

Chapter Nineteen

Zamira had never been more thankful of her private courtyard as she sat on the edge of gray and red mosaic tiles laid out in an intricate pattern around a pond, the bottom of her legs and bare feet dangling in the cool water, while an overturned urn trickled with the sweet sound of running water.

Though half the furnishings inside the palace had been sold off, the bare bones of the palace still revealed a quality that was undeniable.

It was so peaceful and serene in the courtyard, exactly what she needed after reading the newspapers not even an hour ago. Seeing Aziz and Nadia's names in every headline, their faces splashed on every cover, had made her nauseous, her lungs squeezed so tight she had barely been able to breathe.

She recalled the headlines word for word.

Did love win the war?

Is this a royal match?

Two nations united. Peace now reigns.

The photos of Aziz holding Nadia's hand and smiling at her like she was his whole world wasn't something she wanted to think about. And yet she couldn't stop doing exactly that.

She'd once imagined she might be that to him. Then he'd gone and stomped on her heart and left her bleeding out.

A tread sounded behind her and she turned to see her dad approach. She smiled. "Dad. What are you doing here?"

"Can't I spend some time with my only child?"

"Of course. But if it's about Rahim I'm not interested. The war is over, there is no reason now for me to—"

"It's not about him. If I'm being honest I'm glad he didn't become your husband. Not knowing what I do now."

She didn't want to know what he knew, she was certain it wouldn't be anything good. "Then what is it?"

"I'm worried about you. Ever since you left Aziz—"

"Have you ever heard of a captive being released early? He took me against my will, then abandoned me against my will. Now he's marrying a woman I thought he'd never love."

"He doesn't love her," her father said gently. He sat beside her, his knees creaking before he stuck his sandaled feet into the water with a splash. "And he's marrying her for you. It is you he loves, after all."

"If he felt that way it'd be *me* he married."

"And put his people's lives at risk by marrying into a war? What sort of a sheikh would that make him? He sacrificed his heart at the expense of his conscience."

"Am I selfish for wishing he'd followed his heart and not his head?"

"No, not selfish. Not when you love him as much as he loves you."

She stared at him, at his knowing, fatherly concern, his graying beard and wise eyes. His weathered face that showed all the hardships he'd lived through, his own sacrifices he'd made. "How did you know?"

He winced. "I was in love once too. Your mother was an amazing woman. So forward for her time."

She gaped. "I thought she must have been a paragon of virtue, a quiet and cultured woman."

Her father laughed. "No. You are very much like her. And now I'm ashamed that I never shared anything about her to you." He sighed heavily. "It was just too painful, too raw. That you look just like her as well has been a blessing and a curse."

"I had no idea."

He reached out and squeezed her hand. "You have been my greatest joy. I only regret pushing you onto a man who was nowhere near good enough for you."

"The war—"

"Shouldn't have involved you. It wasn't your war to fight."

Tears pricked her eyes. He had had never been this open with her. Though he obviously cared about her, she'd never really felt loved. Not like she did now.

"Your mother would have torn strips off me for what I did. It took Aziz to kidnap you and for me to see the real Rahim to admit my mistake."

Like ripping off a plaster, she suddenly had to know. "What did Rahim do?"

"He showed his true self." He dad shook his head. "He's no gentleman. He's a monster. When I told him you'd been kidnapped, he went into a rage and shot three of his own men."

She clapped a hand to her mouth. "He didn't?"

Her father nodded. "He did. I knew then I had to find a way to get you out of the agreement. Thankfully, Aziz solved that problem by agreeing to marry Nadia."

"So you're saying he saved me from a loveless marriage by committing to a loveless marriage himself?"

"Pretty much. Rest assured though, Nadia will do everything in her power to make him fall in love with her."

Her heart squeezed at the thought. "I can't let that happen," Zamira said softly.

Her father cocked his head to one side. "What did you say?"

She held her father's stare and repeated loudly, "I can't let that happen."

He smiled. "You really are just like your mother." He stretched his legs out. "If it helps, I heard he recently left Sheikh Idris and Nadia's country."

Already? Hadn't she read in one of the many articles that he'd only just arrived there?

She leaned over and hugged him. "Thanks, Dad."

He chuckled, then sobering, he said, "I should never have interfered. You would be blessed to find the kind of love I had with your mother."

"Even if war is brought back to our country?"

He sighed heavily. "Even then." He reached up and touched her face. "Just remember, love always conquers hate."

Tears were streaming down her face when she said, "I hope you're right."

"I know I am."

He was still sitting in the pond when she got up and left him to pack a bag before she'd take their private helicopter to Mukaite.

It was time to confess to Aziz how she really felt...before it was too late.

Zamira packed one suitcase, then threw some more clothes into another bag in the hope she'd extend her stay. But first she'd have to persuade Aziz not to marry Nadia.

Surely Zamira and Aziz's shared history was undeniable? He'd been her first kiss, her first—and only—crush. She just wished she'd recognized her true feelings, but she'd been stubborn and naive.

She knew better now. She didn't want to live with regret for the rest of her lonely life.

She wanted to live a long and fulfilling life.

She wanted a happily ever after with Aziz.

It wasn't until she'd zipped up her luggage that the distinct *whop whop whop* of helicopter rotors sounded from the distance and quickly grew louder.

Her father must have arranged her transport. She smiled. He was really coming through for her.

She hoisted the straps of her luggage over her shoulders. She'd have to sit down with her dad one day soon and chat with him some more about her mother. But first she had her own love life to sort out.

She only hoped it wasn't too little too late.

She hurried to the wing of the palace where stairs led to the roof helipad.

The helicopter had just landed with a roar when she burst through the door, only to discover a distinctly colored, burnt-orange chopper. She froze. That wasn't her father's personal, blue-black bird. Not even close.

Her mouth fell open as Aziz stepped out from the pilot's seat and ducked low, his eyes immediately connecting and holding hers. Her heart thumped in response, her stare taking her fill of him even though disbelief and hope poured through her.

The rotors slowed as he stepped toward her, his thobe flapping around him. The noise had abated by the time he stopped right in front of her and asked, "You're leaving?"

She glanced at the bags, then dropped them to the floor. "Not anymore."

He hesitated. "You're not still seeing Rahim?"

She blinked, caught off guard. Did he seriously think she'd go back on her word? She shook her head. "I was flying over to see you. At least, I thought I was. But here you are."

His eyes darkened. "You were?"

She guessed it wasn't every day a captive voluntarily returned to their captor. But she didn't try to explain, not when a sob tore free and she threw herself into his arms.

He held onto her as though he'd never let her go. "What is it? What's wrong?"

She drew back, her eyes holding his. "Tell me you're not marrying Nadia."

He shook his head. "No, I'm not marrying Nadia."

A tear leaked free. "Then nothing is wrong," she croaked out.

"Yet you're crying."

"Happy tears," she said with a sniffle. She sucked in a steadying breath, then added, "I thought my dad's helicopter had landed to take me to Mukaite, only to find you've arrived here instead."

He smiled. "Seems I saved you the trouble of flying."

She nodded, then blinked up at him as the rotors continued spinning slower and slower. "Why *are* you here?"

"I'm here because I realized I made a terrible mistake."

"Kidnapping me?"

"No. I'd do that all over again to make you see Rahim is not the man for you." He exhaled heavily. "My terrible mistake was thinking I could go through marrying Nadia."

"You're saying you can't?" she asked, joy and a whole lot of other emotions suspended inside her until she knew with absolute certainty what—who—he wanted.

"When I was with her all I thought about was you."

She pressed a shaky hand to her heart. But she couldn't put all her trust in him just yet. "I saw photos of you holding Nadia's hand and looking as though you were in love. There are even headlines about love winning the war and a royal match with two nations united."

He shrugged. "I tried, I really did. I didn't even last twenty-four hours." His smile was a little crooked when he added, "The next newspaper article to come out will be my statement about Nadia and I deciding we're better off as friends."

Zamira felt a little faint as adrenaline and joy began to pour through her. "Really?"

"Yes, really. I walked the streets of Idris' city, searching for the perfect jewelry shop before I returned to my helicopter and flew straight here." He withdrew a square velvet box from a pocket in his thobe, flicking open its lid to reveal a shiny diamond ring, he dropped onto a bent knee. Looking up at her, he asked, "I love you, I've always loved you. Will you marry me, *albi*?"

She couldn't breathe let alone talk. *My heart*. He hadn't been lying when he'd first called her that, she'd just needed to believe him. She sucked in a breath and said, "Yes!"

When he slid the ring on her finger, her breath caught in her throat. "It's a perfect fit," she said, her vision blurring.

"It is," he agreed softly.

He pushed back onto his feet, his head swooping low before his mouth closed over hers. She closed her eyes and soaked up the moment. She'd missed this, missed him. Kissing him was everything right in the world, his hands that held her close reminding her of how secure and protected he made her feel.

He pulled back with a tortured sounding groan and said, "I need to find your father and ask his permission for your hand in marriage."

She withheld a giggle. He couldn't know that her father regretted keeping her away from true love. "I'm sure he'll be more than amenable." She bit her bottom lip. "But what about the possibility of war? I don't want your people being dragged into a conflict."

He nodded. "I spoke to Idris before I left and warned him that he wouldn't be taking on me alone if he was to resume his warfare. My brothers wouldn't hesitate to step in and defend what is mine." He chuckled darkly. "He didn't need to know I wouldn't involve any of my family. The threat was enough." He winced. "I only wish I'd intimidated him sooner."

"So do I," she said softly.

He ran a hand along the back of her head. "We've got the rest of our lives to make up for lost time."

Epilogue

Three weeks later...

Zamira woke slowly, stretching carefully as muscles she didn't even know she had protested at the movement. But it was a good protest. She smiled sleepily. Her husband—as of late yesterday—hadn't just spoken loving vows to her; he'd shown her in every way how much he loved her.

"How are you feeling, Mrs. Al-Hadid?" Aziz asked drowsily, but with a hint of dark possessiveness in his tone.

"Like I've been thoroughly—"

"Loved?" he interjected with a throaty chuckle.

"I was going to say fucked, but your version is much nicer. I think you might be a closet romantic, Mr. Al-Hadid."

"I'm not known to give away my emotions, but I can't hold them back when I'm with you."

She ran a hand over his chest and down his strong abs. "I feel a need to pinch myself and check I'm not dreaming. I thought you'd become such an asshole, but I couldn't have been more wrong. Even before you showed me the orphanage, that you cared so much about your people made me see you weren't a bad person."

"My motive hadn't just been to talk you out of marrying Rahim. I wanted you to become aware of my good side, but then I found myself reluctant having to prove myself. I wanted you to uncover that side of me without any fanfare."

"You didn't need to show me," she said huskily. "You're a great man. And behind every great man is a great woman."

"You're greater in front of me," he whispered tenderly. "You are the love of my life, my darling wife. My heart."

"And you are mine," she said, her voice wobbling with all the emotion building within, the same emotion she saw reflected in his eyes, heard in his voice, felt in every cell in his body.

Love hadn't just shone through and brought them back together like moths to a light. Love had won in the end for them both.

~~~
~~~

Want more Sons of the Sheikh stories by Mel Teshco...?

Falcon

His strike is as sharp as his intellect

Sheikh Raja Hadi might love his province, but he doesn't much care about the politics and legislations in running it. He'd much prefer hanging out with his falcons—the very same bird that has become his nickname—than sitting in the great hall of his palace solving his people's every dispute.

Using cameras mounted on his falcons, the last thing he expects is for a western woman to capture his attention. After observing her for days, he realizes he must have her with or without her consent.

After her cheating boyfriend breaks her heart, Dolly Clark leaves her homeland of Australia and heads to the Middle East. She wants to go someplace faraway, somewhere with a different culture, a different perspective and far different people. What she doesn't expect is to be kidnapped by a stalker with his seeing-eye falcon. Even less expected is her attraction toward him or her growing feelings.

But no matter how tempted she is by him, surely nothing and no one can rebuild her trust in men?

Chapter One of Wedlocked

Sabrina

The euphoria slipping over me like a second skin was nothing short of liberating as I sashayed my way through throngs of glittering guests, surreptitiously eavesdropping on their conversations while I sipped on overpriced bubbles.

I was born for this subterfuge...for the thrill of the hunt. Except, I was no hunter, I wasn't even a spy. Hell, I wasn't even meant to be here tonight.

I was Sabrina Costa, the one and only daughter of the Costa mafia family. Not only was I invaluable, a pawn to my family, I'd become somewhat invisible, too. I could put up with being a pawn—weren't we all?—but it grated my gears that I'd never been allowed to bask in the power and prestige given freely to my brother, Salvatore.

I was determined that would change tonight and I'd be the one who'd uncover what was really going down with our rival mobster family, the Agostinos.

A shiver of unease threatened to take away my swagger. If my father or my brother caught me here at our rival's house, I'd never be without a guard again. Hell, there was a chance I mightn't even make it out of this party alive, if my own family didn't kill me first.

The knowledge sent my pulse racing, my breath catching in the throat. A smile curled my lips. Damn, it was good to finally feel alive! Being groomed to be the next bride to some Frankenstein mobster wasn't my one and only objective in life. *That* was pretty much last on my bucket list.

I was determined to prove one way or another that I wasn't just a pretty face. I had power too, along with connections, they were just more...subtle. I touched my plump, lower lip. One didn't need to fire a semi-automatic when poisoned lipstick could do the job with so much more...finesse.

Not that I was planning on killing anyone tonight. Information was all I desired. After all, information was power and I craved that rush like nothing else, craved to experience what my brother did on a daily basis.

Being a woman hadn't curbed my killer instincts, if anything it'd honed them sharper. I wasn't a behind-the-scenes type of woman, I never had been. I might have been homeschooled and kept socially inept, but it hadn't dulled my brain. My teachers had quickly learned I was bright. Too bright at times for the social role I'd one day soon be forced to play—an arranged marriage to propel my mafia family's standing to the top of the heap once and for all.

I had a fair idea now which man out of the three other mobster families my father planned to assign me to, and it most certainly wouldn't be one of the Agostino brothers. My dad was already leaning toward the Accardi family underboss, anything to push back the powerful Agostino uprising.

I'd be fed to the wolves, quite literally, my virtue of no importance once my father agreed upon my worth. That I was a beauty along with being an innocent would no doubt increase my potential groom-to-be's desire to have me...to own me. And probably hurt me. It would be considered a small price to pay so that my family could wrestle back mobster dominance.

Little wonder I'd been guarded so stringently. My role as daughter had been just as important, possibly more so, than the role of my brother. It meant I'd had few friends or social interactions growing up and I'd had to strive to be adept in a crowd, playing it cool when inwardly my ego and passionate nature battled with my fragile insecurities and inexperience with social engagements.

The one benefit from my upbringing was that no one recognized me now. I was a stranger here, slipping through the party like a wraith in my wraparound, red sheaf dress and silver heels. I'd ensured my striking platinum blonde hair, a trait I shared with Salvatore, was pulled off my face in a braided topknot. I hadn't had time to do much of anything else. Even my lipstick had been applied hastily in the back of the cab I'd ordered to pick me up a block away from my family home.

The Agostinos lived an hour west of New York City, their house overlooking the same Promenade River that my family's house did. Except us Costas lived an hour east of New York. It didn't stop the turf rivalry between us. It was legendary and spanned generations thanks to our forebears who'd moved from Sicily with nothing but a gun, and whole lot of grit and determination.

"I hear Ethan won't be joining us for at least another hour."

My ears pricked at the name of the Agostino underboss, and I tuned into the gossip ensuing between the three young, designer clad women dripping with jewels and barely withheld envy.

"He's celebrating privately first, if you get my drift," said a brunette, her sparkly diamond clips holding back the sides of her dead-straight hair.

Celebrating *what*, exactly? A pity I couldn't approach and straight out ask them. Not without drawing attention to myself.

"Surely there are enough girls willing to do him for free?" a dark-haired women asked, her hands fluttering as she fanned her flushed face. "Lord knows I'd do him in a heartbeat."

"Who says he wants them willing?" the brunette asked with a husky, evocative laugh. "Besides, you'd do anyone for free," she added with a malicious sniff.

I didn't hang around to hear the rest of their mean dialogue, instead I found myself drifting around the huge marble staircase while my thoughts also drifted. I only hoped my platinum wig, which I'd left lying on top of my pillow on my bed back home, would trick anyone who might look in on me until I returned home.

It'd be unlikely anyone would bother. It wasn't like I had a mother anymore to care about me and my father most certainly didn't. As for my brother, our bond was seriously close but even he was too busy lately in his role as our father's underboss to focus on me.

No one would miss me until morning.

In the meantime I had to be careful not to engage in conversation with anyone while being mindful my distinctive hair stayed pulled back so that I didn't stand out. Another frisson of excitement sparked through me as I edged through the crowd. I was just another beautiful face amongst these wealthy and overdressed guests.

The fact I might be one of the few women here without a clutch purse or cellphone was probably more noticeable than my hair. It'd been worth it though just so that I had no identification on me, no proof to get me caught out.

This is stupid! Reckless. Dangerous.

"And I wouldn't change a thing," I murmured to myself as I rounded the grand staircase with its glittering chandelier hanging high above.

I stopped as I inadvertently stumbled upon a discreet service entry elevator, where a harried young waiter pushed a cart of liquor and other supplies inside, the doors then sliding shut behind him.

My belly fluttered and my womb clenched. Was that where I'd find the underboss? Ethan might not yet be the don, but it would only be a matter of time before he took over from his father.

I shuddered. Ethan's father, Lorenzo, made my own dad look like Prince Charming. Violence might be a way of life for our families, but Lorenzo was as soulless as a man could get without already being in hell.

Even I'd heard rumors about the Agostino don's proclivities. He enjoyed inflicting pain and punishment, and got off on watching others suffer. Not even his family was safe. I could only imagine the sadistic children he'd raised.

The elevator doors reopened and a suited man stepped out. His dark eyes trawling over my silver-blonde hair, he asked, "You're here for Ethan?"

I blinked, then automatically nodded as realization kicked in. The soldier presumed I'd been hired to have sex with his boss. I ran an absent hand along the silky fabric of my short, fitted gown. I hadn't intended to dress like one of Ethan's whores, but who was I to deny fate? I wanted answers, what better way to get them than straight from the horse's mouth.

The suited man's eyes glinted. "I can see now why he has a thing for blondes. That lucky bastard really is celebrating tonight."

I managed a coy smile. *Fuck.* Did high-priced whores act cheap or did they swan around like celebrities? The whores that my dad and brother had brought into our home hadn't exactly been subtle about their intentions. But surely discretion was what a higher-end escort provided?

I sashayed past suited-man and stepped alone into the elevator, my panties already a little damp just thinking about what could happen upstairs with Ethan if I wasn't careful. He'd be expecting pre-celebration sex, probably hardcore stuff only the most experienced of women would know how to enjoy.

I swallowed as the doors slid shut and the elevator swept me upstairs. I'd seen pictures of Ethan. He might have been good looking if not for his hard eyes and the jagged white scar spreading halfway along his jaw. If his full lower lip hinted at sexuality, the thin upper lip hinted at cruelty.

He was something of a paradox to me even before the elevator doors slid open and I was greeted with the man himself...in all his naked glory.

Ethan

I lounged back in one of my parlor's many cushioned seats, my dick giving a half-interested spasm as one blonde whore bent over another on the daybed and snorted a thin white line of crank from her hairless pussy. The two women could be sisters for all I knew. They had the same big, enhanced tits and lips, the same sapphire blue eyes and toned, golden bodies with identical pierced clits.

I was tempted to sample some crank from both their pussies to see which one got me highest, but I needed to keep a clear and cool head if I was to face the guests later with my usual dominant control. Even in my own extended family there were those who hoped I'd fail while they climbed a rung or two on the ladder along the way.

I'd ensure those same people hit rock bottom and stayed there while those who wished me the best or helped me triumph were rewarded accordingly.

I drew a hand up and down my dick. Speaking of reward...it was time these blondes got me off. I might be sporting a hard-on, but that was nothing new. I was perpetually hard and ready to fuck at a moment's notice, even when my interest was only half in the game.

I waved a hand at the whores to take me in their mouths. Two tongues dancing along my erection were always better than one. Just as one mouth sucking me, followed by another, always made me come harder.

I'd already watched them tongue each other's pierced clits before they'd come with little shrieks, their arousals scenting the air and sticking in a filmy dew to their inner thighs. It had taken everything I had not to ram my dick into one of their saturated pussies. But if I lost all discipline with a woman, who said my next loss of self-control wouldn't come at the expense of my life?

In my business, control was everything.

I closed my eyes as one of the whores sucked the considerable length of my dick. I thrust a brutal hand through her hair to help dictate her up-down motion. She gasped, her distress all too clear. That it turned me on made me loathe myself almost as much as it intensified my arousal.

Not everyone agreed with my dark desires. Not even these whores I paid a small fortune to please me.

The elevator doors pinged as they opened once again. I smiled, but didn't bother opening my eyes. I enjoyed putting on a show for the harassed wait-staff. A perverse part of me wanted to remind them of my authority and clout, of my sexual dominance. It didn't hurt my reputation, either.

The other whore, who'd been licking and sucking my engorged nuts, stopped suddenly, unprofessionally, to snipe, "Who the fuck is *she*?"

The way she said it in an aggrieved, envious voice caused my eyes to snap open. My hand involuntarily clenched in her friend's already ravaged scalp as my breath stalled deep in my throat.

The woman inside the elevator wasn't just anyone. She was an angel sent from heaven, or at the very least, an angel sent straight out of my wet dreams into my present reality.

Surely she wasn't one of the blonde whores sent to keep me happy tonight? Not even the exclusive, high-priced agency that was one of my family's many businesses had a girl like this one. Was she new? She was most definitely exquisite. I couldn't take my eyes or mind off her, not even when the whores took turns sucking my dick.

From her platinum blonde hair to her silver-gray eyes brimming with intelligence, and her slender physique with tits that were barely restrained inside her dress, she was—

A groan wrenched from my throat as a shockwave tore through my body, then forcibly ejaculated out of me. All thanks to the vision standing in front of me.

Not by the suctioning, practiced rhythm and pressure of the whores' mouths on me. I got blow jobs on a regular basis and was cynical enough to recognize I'd been getting too much of a good thing, like an addict needing more drugs to neutralize the craving.

I released my grip on the whore's hair. That she was professional enough not to wince or gag thanks to the huge load I'd poured down her throat was a credit to her. Once she'd licked me clean, I nodded carelessly at the other whore to do the same, my gaze not once leaving the angel who stood gaping at me from the elevator.

I should probably feel...something. Regret, perhaps? But I'd long ago refused to be weighed down by emotion of any kind, not even in front of a woman who'd jumped straight out of my fantasies.

Only when the whores straightened, no doubt assuming they'd finished their duties for the night, did I then nod at the dark-haired man who stood in the far corner of the parlor. That Evander was also my younger half-brother and a trusted capo was neither here nor there. He might have enjoyed the voyeuristic show, but he loved to fuck, too.

"They're yours now, Evander. Share them with the other men. Ensure everyone gets some action. I do not want to be disturbed for the next hour."

Evander nodded, his broad shoulders clenching beneath his Armani jacket and his brilliant stare gleaming as he herded the naked blondes out of the parlor and into some other area of the house where he and the men would have some fun.

I barely noticed them leave. All my focus remained on the angel who had yet to step out of the elevator and into the room with me. She was a heady mix of shy and emboldened, the tip of her pink tongue moving out to lick her full, crimson lips.

My dick jerked and thickened once again, and my voice came out like sandpaper when I asked, "You're not from our agency, are you?"

Her eyes flashed. "Why else would I be here?"

"Why indeed," I murmured. I glanced past her delectable body to her empty hands. "A hooker without a clutch bag filled with paraphernalia. Am I missing something?"

Her face blanched, but then she smiled and I was too distracted to act on her flash of guilt. "Of course you're missing something," she crooned.

"Oh?"

She bent her legs and swept her hands down and out, showcasing her legs that were as perfectly proportioned as the rest of her. "You've been missing out on me," she answered huskily.

She wasn't wrong. Where *had* she been all my life? Yet irrational disappointment bit deep even as satisfaction settled over me. I wanted her to be the innocent, naïve woman who enchanted and fixated me, even as I wanted her to be the whore I could fuck into submission until her cries filled my ears and my seed filled her empty crevices.

"Come here," I commanded.

After a momentary pause, she stepped out of the elevator and into my parlor, my dick lifting like a snake in front of her hungry stare. I smirked. Oh yes, she wanted me, her innocent demeanor offset by a passionate nature she hadn't quite managed to repress.

My engorged dick throbbed with painful need, as though I'd not just blown my load a few minutes earlier. "Dress off. Now."

She blinked, the faint tremor in her hands the only indication of nerves. "It doesn't work that way, not with me," she said huskily.

Shock for a moment held me in its grip. Since when did a whore tell me how things worked? I commanded and they obeyed. Yet a part of me was stimulated by her defiance, aroused by a need to dominate and fuck her into complete capitulation.

The pulse at her throat surged, and suddenly I wanted to bite her there before kissing away the sting. I wanted to taste and lick and bite every part of her body, while inhaling her scent until she became a part of me.

Holy fuck. I hadn't been this stimulated since...forever. But it didn't mean I'd let her waltz in here like she ran the fucking show.

"*You're* telling *me* how it works in *my* home at *my* party?" I asked. "Do you know who I am?"

She nodded. "I know exactly who you are, *Ethan Agostino*." She stopped in front of me, and I inhaled her amber notes with fruity peach undertones, like the scent had been made especially for her. *Damn.* This whore had done her homework, knew how a unique scent like hers drove me half-crazed with lust.

My dick bucked, the skin on my shaft pulled so damn tight I wondered if I might embarrass myself and lose all that control I prided myself on. "So how *does* it work?" I asked, giving into the treacherous desire to see exactly what she was playing at.

"You ask me to do something, then you have to reciprocate in return," she said huskily, her voice rich honey poured over a delicate bite of velvety, dark chocolate.

"So take off your dress," I instructed, "then I might reciprocate."

Her silver-gray eyes turning molten, she tugged at the little bow on the side of her dress that drew the fabric tight around her waist, delineating it. Only once the fabric loosened did she draw the gown up and over head, exposing her gorgeous body in a crimson lace thong and matching bra that barely contained her plump, ripe tits.

I lowered my gaze, my mouth drying at the narrow, platinum blonde tuft of hair just visible through the triangular bit of lace that made up her tiny thong. She was a natural blonde. Even her pale skin was flawless, except for the fine white scar embedded on her hip. I frowned, tempted to ask about it, needing to know everything about her past, present and her future.

Because as sure as I'd be crowned don in the next hour, I knew she had to be a part of my future. I'd force her if necessary. She was already my employee, it wouldn't be too difficult coercing her to be my mistress for as long as she continued to excite and arouse me.

Taking was what I did. I saw no reason to stop now.

She was mine.

If you'd like to know when my next book is available, as well as pre-orders, cover reveals and other news, sign up for my newsletter:

Check out my website – http://www.melteshco.com/

You can also friend me on Facebook at https://www.facebook.com/mel.teshco

Or my author Facebook page at https://www.facebook.com/MelTeshcoAuthor

Contact me: melteshco@yahoo.com.au

If you enjoy my books I'd be delighted if you would consider leaving a review. This will help other readers find my books ☺

About the Author

I'm an award winning author who loves to write scorching hot contemporary and science fiction romance—stories I love to read. I love working from home, where my office window looks out over our 'block' of fourteen acres with gorgeous mountain views. After enjoying a stint as a foster carer for cats, I now have seven felines to entertain me, along with two dogs and two horses. But only when I'm not distracted by my three gorgeous daughters, one of whom—a teenager *shriek*—is still living at home. As for my husband...he's still waiting for retirement.

Want more Mel Teshco books?

Contemporary

Sons of the Sheikh

Scorpion (book 1)

Falcon (book 2)

Wolf (book 3)

Leopard (book 4)

Jackal (book 5)

Desert Kings Alliance

The Sheikh's Runaway Bride (book 1)

The Sheikh's Captive Lover (book 2)

The Sheikh's Forbidden Wife (book 3)

The Sheikh's Secret Mistress (book 4)

The Sheikh's Defiant Princess (book 5)

The Sheikh's Fake Fiancée (book 6)

The Sheikh's Royal Widow (book 7)

The Sheikh's Temporary Girlfriend (book 8)

Desert Kings Alliance Box Set (Volumes 1-4)

Desert Kings Alliance Box Set (Volumes 5-8)

Gangsters at War

Wedlocked (book 1)

Avenged (book 2)

Enforced (book 3)

Contracted (book4)

Reformed (book 5)

Unresolved (book 6)

Bachelor Brothers of Sydney

Highest Bid (book 1)

Bought at Auction (book 2)

Winning Offer (book 3)

The VIP Desire Agency

Lady in Red (book 1)

High Class (book 2)
Exclusive (book 3)
Liberated (book 4)
Uninhibited (book 5)
The VIP Desire Agency Boxed Set (all 5 books in the series)
Box sets with authors Christina Phillips & Cathleen Ross
Sheikhs & Billionaires
Taken by the Sheikh
Taken by the Billionaire
Taken by the Desert Sheikh
Resisting the Firefighter
Standalone longer length titles: (50k-100k)
As I Am
Standalone novellas and short stories: (15k-40K)
Her Dark Guardian
Stripped
Clarissa
Camilla
Selena's Bodyguard (also part of the Christmas Assortment Box)
Anthologies
Down and Dusty: The Complete Collection
The Christmas Assortment Box
Science Fiction
The Virgin Hunt Games
The Virgin Hunt Games volume 1
The Virgin Hunt Games volume 2
The Virgin Hunt Games volume 3
The Virgin Hunt Games volume 4
The Virgin Hunt Games volume 5
The Virgin Hunt Games volume 6
Alien Fugitives
Nero (book 1)

Jasper (book 2)
Sienna (book 3)
Damaris (book 4)
Dragons of Riddich
Kadin (prequel - book 1)
Asher (book 2)
Baron (book 3)
Dahlia (book 4)
Wyatt (book 5)
Valor (book 6)
The Queen (book 7)
Alien Hunger
Galactic Burn (book 1)
Galactic Inferno (book 2)
Galactic Flame (book 3)
Coming soon
Galactic Blaze (book 4)
Nightmix
Lusting the Enemy (book 1)
Abducting the Princess (book 2)
Seducing the Huntress (book 3)
Winged & Dangerous
Stone Cold Lover (book 1)
Ice Cold Lover (book 2)
Red Hot Lover (book 3)
Winged & Dangerous Box Set (all 3 books in the series)
Dirty Sexy Space continuity with Denise Rossetti:
Yours to Uncover (book 1)
Mine to Serve (book 6)
Ours to Share (book 8)
Awakenings series with Kylie Sheaffe
No Ordinary Gift (book 1)

Believe (book 2)
Homecoming (book 3)
Standalone longer length titles: (50k-100k)
Dimensional
Mutant Unveiled
Shadow Hunter
Existence
Standalone novellas and short stories: (15k-40K)
Identity Shift
Moon Thrall
Blood Chance
Carnal Moon